AFTER THE VIKINGS

TALES OF FUTURE MARS

by
G. David Nordley

illustrated by Wolf Read

AFTER THE VIKINGS

Brief Candle
Press

Publishing History
Earlier versions of the stories in this book appeared as follows:
"Morning on Mars" appeared in *Analog Science Fiction/Fact*, Davis Publications, June 1992.
"The Day of Their Coming" appeared in *Asimov's Science Fiction Magazine*, Dell Magazines, March 1994
"Comet Gypsies" appeared in *Asimov's Science Fiction Magazine*, Dell Magazines, March 1995
"A Life on Mars" appeared in *Analog Science Fiction/Fact*, Dell Magazines, July/August 1998
"Martian Valkyrie" appeared in *Analog Science Fiction/Fact*, Dell Magazines, January 1996

All other material is original to this work and is printed with permission of the author and publisher.

First published in 2013 by Variations on a Theme

Cover design: Brief Candle Press

First Brief Candle Press edition published 2015
www.briefcandlepress.com

ISBN: 978-1-942319-02-3

This book is dedicated to the memory of
Willy Ley, G. Harry Stine, and Poul Anderson

TABLE OF CONTENTS

PREFACE

THE FIRST EDITORS of this short collection were Stanley Schmidt and Gardner Dozois, who bought these stories for *Analog Science Fiction/Science Fact* and *Asimov's Science Fiction* respectively, and who helped me make them better stories in the process.

The original occasion for this collection was CONTACT XIV, the fourteenth annual interdisciplinary conference on the possible evolution of and encounter with extraterrestrial intelligence. CONTACT is not concerned with ballistic crockery. It gathers engineers, writers, anthropologists, scientists, artists and others who dream of the Great Out There and share our dreams of a spacegoing civilization to be. Extraterrestrials are a focus and reason for being of the conference, but the participants include in that term the people who will live beyond the Earth as well.

Mars became a natural focus for that year's conference. Fossils of what appear to be primitive life forms were found in meteors that unquestionably were chipped off Mars in one of its many encounters with the nearby asteroids. It seemed a good occasion to recycle my Mars stories, to have something to contribute to the general Mars theme of the conference. My good friend, Wolf Read, offered to do the artwork. Except for a couple of minor additions, all the interior artwork herein is from him.

In the original draft, the stories were assembled in the chronological order of their writing, not that of their future history. As I assembled them, I realized that I had written them in exactly the reverse of their future historical order. This archeological discovery of my own past suggested a light-hearted frame to tie the stories together. So, for a page or two in front of each story, you will find a pair of alien archeologists, Hive-Father Althor and his Eldest Daughter, peeling back of layers of sediment from the latest and earliest story, "Morning on Mars," to the earliest and latest, "Martian Valkyrie." In between are a first contact story, "The Day of their Coming" which echoes both major themes of CONTACT XIV; a story of Martian terraforming, "Comet Gypsies," which does not actually take place on Mars but concerns an absolutely essential part of it, and, "A Life on Mars," which was written subsequent to the CONTACT draft of the collection and added into the appropriate time slot, along with its interstory material.

G. David Nordley, Sunnyvale 2013

AROUND AN ANCIENT STAR

HIVE-LORD ALTHOR caressed his eldest daughter and urged her over to the viewport to look at the ruddy, dusty world below them.

"God-awful ancient world," he hissed, both overtones and undertones carrying meaning. "It's been around that white dwarf some seven or eight billion times, I'd say. God knows how many civilizations have been through here."

"If there is such a being, He might. We are newcomers, and I'm certain there's more to this galaxy, out there," she waved a feathered ear toward the infinite, "watching us."

"We could bioform it. It's held life before. There's enough material in the moons of those Giant Planets. Not much of an asteroid belt left, though."

"It's a new white dwarf, fading rapidly. In a million revolutions, it won't provide enough light."

"That, daughter, is a long time." Althor did a quick mental calculation — about a hundred times longer than their race had written records.

"Well, bioforming it can wait until we finish our excavations. The last people to live here were avians — huge beaks, big heads, smallish bodies and big wings. About two billion revolutions ago — with this high axial tilt, there are a lot of annual weather phenomena that leave layers — we can count the revolutions. The atmosphere must have been much thicker then."

"Quite right. Blasted away by the red giant phase of this star. If we'd only gotten here a hundred million revolutions or so earlier. The star must have started out in the yellow class — not as bright as it is now, but much bigger and more yellow. Hard to see how it had a thick atmosphere, though, exposed to the solar wind as such."

"But it did, and several times. Look at all the dry riverbeds, the eroded volcanoes, and the newer ones."

"Still bubbling a little then?"

"A little. It takes a long time for heat to build up enough to make it burp. But I think it could still happen. There's probably a lot of neat stuff under those lava flows, but we've had our best luck in the shore deposits."

"Near what used to be oceans?"

"A few ropes above the ideal ellipsoid."

"Anything new?"

"Well, for about three billion revolutions before the avians, there were some furry creatures, who could, from their skeletons, move about on two or four limbs. They were," she shrank in disgust "inside-out folk — with their soft parts in a bag of rubbery tissue hung around their hard bones."

"Is that possible?"

Eldest Daughter fluttered flower-like hands at the tip of vine-like arms. "I just told you it was, Father. They liked to carve reliefs of themselves in wood and then encase the wood in diamond — we've found a couple dozen of these trinkets."

"That's all? Diamond coated wood trinkets?"

"Things lost on a beach or in a wood, father. We haven't found a mother shell, a hive, or anything like it. We should if you give us time."

The Hive-Father nodded. Starting a bioforming project now could be premature. "Very well. We can postpone worldbuilding for a little while. We shall build a space hive out of the outer moon, big enough to spin so our pressure tubes don't get weak-walled. You'll have as many revolutions as you need. Maybe you'll find where they went —

they couldn't have just vanished. They had spaceships, spacehives —
why, this system is littered with artifacts going back billions of these
revolutions. What could this planet tell us that *that* doesn't?"

Eldest Daughter warbled in a display of awe. "They have already
told us something; Father, they have told us we are not alone, three
times not alone."

"But the space junk tells us... did you say three times?"

"There is evidence of yet another people here, true bipeds, before
the furry people, when this world was very young..."

"Amazing, but you seem troubled, Eldest Daughter."

"An anachronism. We have found a fossilized skeleton, and very
advanced artifacts with it, in layers where the furry people have only
spears and stones. But tooth marks on the bones match the teeth of
the furry people."

"An easy problem, Daughter. One of those old ones killed the other
and left the furry folk a meal and the blame. A murder, I should say."

Eldest Daughter's tentacles drooped in exasperation at the self-
confidence her Hive-Father showed in his judgment, however far
beyond the data it strayed. "I don't know about a murder, Hive-
Father. But, in those bones, there is at least a story — if you give me
time to read it."

MORNING ON MARS

THE FOREST WAS YOUNG when humanity was old, and now the forest was old.

Tohn contemplated the relativity of young and old as he descended the ancient sky bridge between the moon Deimos and continental Tharsis. The great volcanoes had weathered; he could see a chaos of crags and valleys where the great caldera and lava shield of Ascraeus Mons had once stood.

There would be no more where it came from, he thought. It had still been recognizable before he went to the Andromeda.

Sadness slipped over his mind so much like a shadow over a sun that he shivered — the biochemical heritage of a voluntary, stubbornly determined, living fossil. But a moment of mirth at himself brightened him. He accepted feelings, even knowing whence they came: the exact evolutionary pattern, the type of environment that had conditioned them, however inappropriate. He accepted and enjoyed them in the way his ancestors, and even he, would still take the trouble to build a wood fire in the wilderness with much better means to warm themselves at hand. For racial nostalgia, for remembrance.

He had come to the ancient home system with his companion of the last few millennia, Kairl, whose ancestors had come from the soft green, lake-studded world growing below him. Increasingly distracted, she had left suddenly for home, and he had come to find her. He came the old way, searching in person; for the Mind of Mars, which included her parents, would honor her desire for privacy. But it would also honor his need by not interfering.

The terminus was a well-maintained re-creation of colonial Mars, and, conforming to the chronology of the setting, he used the ancient phonetic language with the automata who served the terminus. He located the sporting equipment dispensary.

"Good morning." He beckoned a slender golden-haired female work of android art in a simple blue robe sitting cross-legged among stacks of the eldritch outdoor paraphernalia. It was actually sewing something. "I'll need a set of wings and goggles. I've come hunting."

"Ha!" it chimed in a clear soprano, and displayed a screen fastener, apparently just reattached. "Could I interest you in a freshly repaired tent as well?"

His body was a conservative genetic design, but even so, if he chose to sleep he could do so naked in the snow without discomfort or physical risk. He wore a jumpsuit for social convention, to conserve energy, and for the convenience of pockets. He respected form, but he had not come to simply indulge himself in anachronisms like setting up tents.

"Only slow me down, I'm afraid."

It raised blond eyebrows on a seemingly sculptured Slavic face with high cheeks and thin lips that seemed set in a slight but permanent frown. "Wow, so we're, on a mission are we? Are you natural enough that it might be a woman you're hunting?"

"Well, yes. She might be about to decide to do something which I'd rather she didn't. I want to try to change her mind." And if he was too late, perhaps join her. Wondrous as they are, galaxies, like Beethoven, could bear only so much repetition. How long could *he* go on, just on philosophy, and will, when everything was melting away?

After four million years, his first long-term partner, Ellincy, had joined the Mind of Preathe, her homeworld. It had been time, she told him, for a change. But she would always be in there for him, her mind at his call. She would always care, always remember. He sent to her now, knowing the Mind of Mars would pass his message on, to reach her some ten thousand years from now.

"*That* decision?" the Golden Lady sighed. "You must mean Kairl DiTensio; she was through here three months ago, talking of taking a

last walkabout in the flesh. She headed for the Syrtis hills on foot."
She touched the door of one of the three meter-tall cabinets that lined
her room and it swung open to reveal a tall contraption of thin rods
and iridescent gossamer fabric. The wings might have been plucked
from some gargantuan dragonfly. "Here, these will do nicely. They're
a good compromise between racing and soaring."

Yes, a good choice of wings. He called forth memories, and waited
as details he had left with the Mind of Mars poured back into his
consciousness. Um, the harness goes on *so.* Handgrips and elbow
sockets needed adjustment. He put a primitive but efficient headband
in place and the feeling of having a tail returned. He folded it down
from his back and touched the floor a couple of times in experiment.
Fine. The Golden Lady helped him adjust the handgrips; the last user
had longer arms. In doing so she brushed against him, making him
think that perhaps she wasn't part of the artificially recreated setting
after all.

Are you? he thought, anachronistically forgetting to speak.

"Natural human? Oh yes, mostly." She smiled, making adjust-
ments, tugging here and there on various straps, and continued aloud.
"I liked doing this so much that I made a few changes, so that I could
like it forever." Then, like most others, she had taken some small step
away from human nature for eternal happiness. But apparently a
smaller step than most; she was still flesh and blood. "How long since
you've been on Mars?"

"About eight million years. I returned to Milky Way five millennia
ago with Kairl. I met her at a supernova party in the Andromeda, and
we found we were both from home system, if you can believe that. I
was born at Maxwell City, four hundred fifth century; Tohn Burken
Lloyd-Wu."

"Oh! A couple real old timers we are! I was doing Boreal Ocean
cruises then — Windjammers from Dumont before the Chryse Sea
silted up. I go back to when Andromeda meant a constellation as well
as a Galaxy." She shook her head. "Turn around and both the language and the sky change on you. I'm Ingrid Karinsdotter. Welcome
to Mars in the one hundred and two thousand three hundred and
seventh century! Umm, I think you're all set now. Ten minutes on the
air fountain to get your reflexes back. Rules, you know."

He grinned in anticipation. Flying was fun, and he hadn't done any since Wondersphere, on their way back in, three thousand years ago. Though the air was more dense, gravity was almost four times higher here. The wings were lighter, larger, and more sophisticated, with all kinds of artificial sinews and lock positions to ease the strain.

She sighed and touched his arm. "Stop by when you have more time." Her invitation had no urgency, but promised a warmth of companionship.

"Uh, we might do that." He nodded and headed for the air fountain.

People, he contemplated as he went through the ancient passageways, had built the original version of this handicapped with unmodified fertility, undimmed sexual and territorial urges, as well as short lives. Biological immortality in the twenty-fourth century had required a drastic lowering of the birth rate. Not to zero; accidental deaths still happened and could be replaced.

But for millions of years voluntary discorporation, usually to join the great planetary minds, had reduced the living population faster than it was being replaced; Mars was almost empty now. People, eventually, got bored. He and Ingrid were unusual, she the more so. At least six million of his ten million years had been spent in transit stasis. She had been apparently active, here, the entire time. He would have to ask about her modification; she had somehow edited boredom from herself without compromising a vital personality.

His thoughts went to their ancestors: imagine being internally compelled to mate, men irrationally risking life and fortune like stags in mating season! And the risks of pregnancy for the ancient women! And yet they had built this, distracted every time they looked at each other, losing their lives minute by minute, each doing a little and passing it on. In the light of his inner mind, the spare squarish panels and glass of the terminus took on a heroic majesty. In his travels among seven galaxies, only a dozen races had climbed out of their evolutionary muck. Humanity was a wonder. He jumped into the air fountain.

The reflexes returned rapidly; wings, arms, and tail soon moving in effortless coordination to grab and thrust air, then to soar. When he felt fully confident, he feathered and lit back on the edge of the air fountain. He released and restrapped his wings for practice, and everything was just right.

He checked out a pack, some large comfortable shorts with large comfortable pockets, fishhooks and line, some high energy rations to save him the trouble of hunting and gathering en route, a canteen, and a set of nested cookware.

He also took a compact multisensor, a directional imaging scanner using a variety of wavelengths longer than visual. An imitation of a four hundredth century device, it was compatible with his genuine four hundredth century neural interface. He could close his eyes and see what it saw. The Mind of Mars would not deny him communications or navigation, but he would have to find Kairl himself.

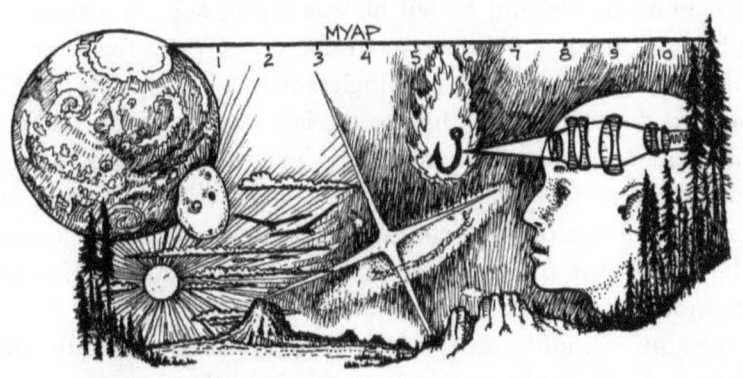

Then, wings restrapped, he was back in the air fountain and out the top. Eyes closed, he spotted the infrared tower of air that was a thermal updraft, and with firm hard strokes arced toward it. He caught it and spiraled up ten thousand feet over the tortured badlands of eroded basalt. Eastward, toward Syrtis, he spotted another thermal and glided toward its base, thinking of Kairl. A full-bodied woman whose jet black hair hung long and straight past her waist, she was both impulsive and mysterious. Often she did not explain, but just *did*.

As they had approached the Solar system, she had become increasingly tense and distracted. When they arrived, he had gone to the comet museum off Eris to gain the perspective of distance on Kairl's moods and to renew his acquaintance with history.

The Pioneers and Voyagers were there, along with the one surviving sphere of the original Beamrider. He had spent a silent hour with the husk of Halley's Comet, long since retired from its blistering sunward journeys. Measured in generations, in the number of lives, it had seen far more human history than he had. If it could only tell him! A hundred of his fellow living fossils had been there, at what had become somewhat of a shrine at the gateway to the Solar System.

Kairl had stayed behind to bask on the dwarf planet's bubble-enclosed surface in the warmth of the gigantic Eris reflector and attend an entertainment festival. One thing had led to another and when he returned a month later than planned, the message had been waiting for him. She had left for Mars, the pull of home stronger than a relationship which was only a few thousand subjective years old. He followed immediately. But he felt he was losing her. Humanity was losing her, too, he thought. She was in that crisis which took so many – the crisis of lost purpose, of meaninglessness.

The next thermal brought him to the lakes and marshes that dotted the former sea basin. A punishing journey on foot, he thought, dangerous, too. suited for one who felt self-destructive. The speed and muscles of a human of his generation could easily overcome a single bear, but there were things which hunted in packs. From the sky too, he remembered and looked around. What's out there?

Those hunt at night, the Mind of Mars reminded him, unbidden, but perhaps he had subconsciously transmitted that last question in his mind. Fear would trigger that.

In a day, he crossed Chryse, now a plain of forests and lakes, coasting from thermal to thermal. In principle, he could have continued — and night was a good time to hunt — but also a good time to be hunted, and with his attention elsewhere, he was an easy mark. In the twilight he stooped toward a clearing among the redwoods on the slopes of the ancient plateau. A stream ran nearby. About fifty meters away was a high bare spot among some large stones. A good campsite.

He hung his wings and pack from a nearby tree and gathered kindling. At this latitude, he was in the lee of the Martian trade winds and things were fairly dry. A thick dry downed branch shattered nicely into small logs when he struck a sharp boulder with it. He made a little log cabin of kindling and logs, stuffing it with dry leaves and twigs. He moved the smaller stones into a circle to contain the fire to be.

A movement in the brush caught his eye. Dog-sized, but it moved like a squirrel. Belatedly, he asked the Mind of Mars for an update on Martian wildlife. A lot can happen in five million years. Large descendants of the gray squirrel, what he had seen moved with equal ease on two or four legs, and had developed an omnivorous diet and simple tool-using behavior. They had retained their large incisors.

Then he looked at his fire to be. And realized he had brought nothing to light it with. Laughing to himself, he took one of the mini-logs and dug a hole in its side with his camp knife. He put the whittlings back in their hole, took another stick and started to spin it when he had an idea.

His four hundredth century brain came with its own fifty watt directional microwave transmitter. He took a fishhook and put it in his hole of chips and shouted at it, *Burn, burn, burn.* Anyone in receiving distance would wonder what he was shouting about, he chuckled.

But nothing happened. He reached for the fishhook in disappointment — and dropped it immediately. Hot. So it was working. Now, if he could only keep this up. Ten minutes later, much more exhausted than he would have been if he had simply twirled his twig, he had a small blaze going. He was congratulating himself when the first rock hit.

He threw it back, harder, and heard it ricochet of trees like distant gunshots. He pegged a few more in the general area, then remembered his sensor, hanging on the tree with his pack and wings. On a hunch, he shut his eyes to see through its lens.

Just in time. Small furry paws were grabbing at it. He opened his eyes and charged with a yell. They vanished. He took his equipment down and moved it closer to the fire.

Okay, Mind of Mars, let's stop playing games, he transmitted. *Did Kairl make it through this far?*

Kairl very firmly told us not to interfere.

What does that mean? Is she still alive?

A pause. *Yes. For now. She says she will see you. She is here.* A topographic map appeared in front of his eyes, and he recognized the basic features. She was less than twenty kilometers away. *But you must hurry. And be very careful yourself.*

He had his wings on in two minutes and with a leap that bore witness to conditioning as well as genetic engineering, was aloft.

Tohn? Her voice as distinctive in radio as audio.

Yes, Kairl. I'm on my way.

This is the way it is. The squirrels have me and I don't want you to interfere. It's hopeless anyway. I was observing them, and saw one of them kill and start eating another's baby. I interfered and they've injured and cornered me. Don't be shocked. I think that I can hold them off until you get here, to say goodbye. I know how you feel about life and I really feel bad about Eris. But I had to make the break then.

He stroked hard, skimming treetops half a kilometer above the ground. *Hey kid*—she was less than a tenth his subjective age—*we've been through a lot and made it. We'll get out of this too. Just hang in there.*

No, Tohn. I'm going to join the Mind, with Mom, Dad, and the rest of my family. Sorry to disappoint you, but it's what I need to do. You know, this is really an interesting way to go, not boring at all. I'm returning my body, nourishing our successors. I don't think I could have planned it so well.

Then he was there. Nothing but treetops, but he could hear squeals and thumps. He stooped through the branches in a sparse area, protecting the wings with his body. He broke through quickly and cleanly and broke his fall with wings locked open, composite fiber sinews taking the strain. Then he glided past the trunks a hundred feet above the ground toward the noise.

In the sensor, in the near infrared, the scene was almost as clear as day. Kairl, her hair glowing with warm blood, backed into a notch of rock, the carcass of a small supersquirrel at her feet, was fending off twenty or so adults with a stout branch. She was being stoned and bleeding badly. She had one leg.

See, her voice laughed, *if I really were an old style human, I'd already be dead. But my wounds don't bleed, my bones don't break easily, and I can shut off the pain. It's great theater, isn't it?*

You will regenerate if I can get you out of there, he pleaded. *Please!*

No, don't try. I am going willingly. This is getting tiresome, and I'm hurting them. I'll have to continue this conversation as part of the Mind of Mars. Talk to you then.

As he watched helplessly, she shouted and advanced toward them, using her stick as a crutch. There was a pause as they momentarily recoiled, and he struggled toward her, the Martian air viscous to his accelerated time sense, hoping to snatch her like an eagle from that small clearing around her.

She saw him, grinned and waved, the mellow burbling music that had graced his life for the past five millennia. A rock struck her head and she crumpled. The stump of her leg bled freely. Then they were upon her and he on them.

He screamed and a few looked up but most were too busy with their bloody incisors.

It's too late, she laughed, *I'm here now, in the Mind of Mars, on Phobos. I'm fine. It's wonderful.*

"But it's not human!" he screamed in both ways. More supersquirrels looked up. So they're sensitive to that? What might be in their genes, he wondered? He remembered his fire-starting technique, and circled, concentrating on a feeder. It put its hands to its head, and fell. He moved to the next one. It fell as well. On the third one, he backed off a little. It reared up and squeaked in terror and the others reared up too. He was conscious of spending his energy at a fantastic rate, flying and shouting. He could now see what was left of Kairl. A supersquirrel went back down to it and he hit it with a furious microwave blast.

Confused, they avoided Kairl's body, but some moved to the carcass of the youngster. He hit those too. Irrational, pointless. There was nothing to save. And suddenly felt weary beyond measure. With the last dregs of his hysterical energy, he glided to a stout lower limb of a great tree, some twenty meters above the forest floor, managed to hang on and hoist himself over it, gasping.

Too tired to move, he noticed, almost disinterestedly, that some of the smaller supersquirrels had waddled over to the base of his tree. One of the smaller supersquirrels moved over to the small carcass, which the others now avoided, and pushed at it. *Its mother?* Tohn asked.

Yes, the Mind of Mars said with Kairl's voice. *See that they are gray colored, and the others have a reddish cast. We think she was captured, mated, and when her child didn't look like the others... Well, I was stupid to get involved,* she declared with the authority of the ten-million-year-old cybersapient of which she was now part.

You were human, Tohn replied, bitterly emphasizing the "were".

The Gray moved to what was left of Kairl, and pushed at that too. It avoided the Reds that Tohn had killed. It looked up at him, clearly sensing, by smell perhaps, his likeness with the being who had tried to save its child.

Do you think they could eventually be civilized? Tohn sent.

It is possible, but it is certainly a very long-term project, the Mind replied, in its own voice. *This group, despite its behavior, is the most intelligent we've seen. They don't have fire, but some of the stones they throw have been edged, by them. They understand sticks and use them for a variety of things, including as a lever. Their social organization is simple domination by the most aggressive member. Analysis shows that at some time in the distant past they received some human genetic material, perhaps as part of a medical experiment. Our knowledge before the twenty-fifth century is not all-inclusive. Also, there has been a lot of environmental change here, operating on ten million years of genetic drift. We suggest you conserve your radio voice; it's very faint now.*

Worn out, Tohn thought; everything was so old. The sun had warmed enough that old Earth, like Venus, needed a sunshield. A year was no longer a year: for the past six million of them giant solar sails had sat alongside Mercury, Venus, and the Earth-Moon system balanced on solar pressure and tugging the planets gently, persistently, outward from the growing Sun with the thin elastic of gravity.

A tug on his leg brought him back to more immediate concerns, and he irritably jerked his leg away, momentarily pleased that he could move it again, though the effort exhausted him. Then he stared at the cause of the tug with a hint of fear. One of the Reds had climbed the tree to reach him, and he was still very weak. Free for a second, he pulled himself about a meter further out on the branch, his arms clearly telling him that neither fight nor flight was possible just yet.

A confusion of motion and squeaks erupted, and a gray furball appeared between him and the Red. Squeals and blood. The shock of events cleared his mind, and he belatedly thought of his rations. He managed to get some from his pockets and stuffed his mouth. It would take minutes for them to do him any good, but better later than never.

An idea. He waited for a lull in the battle of the branch. The Gray had assumed an effective defensive position, and the current Red on the point was hesitating. He got the Gray's attention. It almost snapped at him, but stopped just in time. He bit a chunk off the ration bar and held out the rest to the Gray, who took a hand off the branch without losing its balance, and quickly stuffed the bar into its mouth pouch. It flashed its incisors at a non-serious lunge by the Red.

Another idea. He got the Gray's attention again and showed it his camp knife, slicing a piece of bark in demonstration. The Gray got the idea immediately, and even gave a short chirp. It took the knife and held it in its hand easily. The next half-hearted lunge by the Red earned it a split nose. It emitted a squeal from hell and deserted the point position.

Its replacement didn't lunge. A standoff.

The gunshot startled him, and the Gray shivered in terror, but turned to face the new threat. Two more shots and the Reds were running. Tohn found he could move now, and hoisted himself around, straddling the branch like a saddle. Thus secure he looked around.

A blonde Valkyrie wearing exceptionally thin black wings appeared and flew to the trunk, grasping it in a maneuver that would shame any cat or woodpecker.

"Think we can persuade your lady friend to put down the knife?" Ingrid asked.

♂ ♂ ♂

With fire and the ancient gun to keep the others at bay, they camped near the battle site for three more days. What remained of Kairl, a body which had lived ten times longer than any of the trees around it, and which was destroyed by semisapient barbarians in a few minutes, was burned with reverence, as was that of the fallen Gray pup, possibly less than a Martian year old. Somehow, the Gray mother seemed to understand this, and looked up with them as the smoke wafted skyward. They moved the bodies of the fallen Reds some hundred meters away and left them for the ravens. Servants and

eyes of the Mind of Mars, they could taste the fruits of its noninterfer-
ence policy.

The Gray permitted Ingrid to treat its wounds, and then, surren-
dering all caution with the humans, let itself be stroked and hugged.
There was almost an erotic delight in doing so, in which all three
beings indulged themselves. The Gray purred, like a cat.

Ingrid was impressed by the novelty of Tohn's fire-starting technique, though not by its efficiency. She was even more impressed by
its effect on one of the occasional Red intruders.

"The bioelectronic array was built from genes from the visual system." he told her. His grandfather had been on the project, so its
details were part of a memory he always carried with him. "Morpho-
logically, it's like a huge retina behind the forehead. If I focus my eyes
on a target, and then think of transmitting *through* my eyes, instead
of *at* the target, I get the best concentration."

With practice, Ingrid was able to master the technique. "Has anyone ever done this before?" she wondered aloud.

Not on Mars, or in any other of my records, the Mind answered.
That covered a lot of space-time, but not everything.

"Well, that's close enough to new to excite me!" she exclaimed.
"See, we'll never be old enough to know everything!"

Later, with Tohn's energy restored and the Grays wounds healed,
they flew escort for her back to her own territory. Among her own
kind, after some wary wiggling of noses, she scampered back into her
burrow, then popped her head out and sounded what Ingrid and Tohn
now recognized as a happy chirp. They waved as they flew off. They
went south to the equator for strong westerlies, then west toward
Tharsis.

Now I have something new to show you! Ingrid radiated as they
soared along. *Actually, we've been predicting it for some time, but the
first evidence showed up only the day you left. It's why I went after
you; I thought it might help convince Kairl to hang around a few
more millennia.*

*Whether you like to believe it or not, I'm still here, cruising over
your heads,* the Mind told them in Kairl's voice, *and if you want to
see something else new and exciting, look to the west, on the cloud
deck.*

Tohn saw a dark spot moving toward them with the deceptive slowness of distance. But it would be to them in minutes.

"An eclipse!" Excited, he shouted in both ways. *"I think we can catch it if we fly south a little more."* They did so, then turned back east and gained as much altitude as they could. When the first hint of shadow reached them, they dove, getting as much eastward velocity as possible. When the air turned cold and the sky black, they looked up.

The corona shone. The blue and gray double star of Earth-Moon shown and the brilliant white of Venus.

There's Sirius, Ingrid broadcast. In whatever new constellation, Tohn thought.

Look, to the left of the sun; that must be Mercury, and its solar sail.

Yes, I see it.

Ouch, look away. A brilliant bead flashed into photosphere on Phobos' racing eastern limb. Totality had only lasted a few seconds.

I'm impressed, Tohn declared. *Just how long has this been going on?*

Only for the last few centuries, the Mind of Mars replied, *and you couldn't see it from the surface; Phobos hasn't dropped quite low enough yet. I'm going to maintain its orbit with an electrostatic jet when it's low enough to provide a good show at the surface.*

Will wonders never cease? Tohn meant his question to be rhetorcal, but Ingrid answered anyway.

Just wait until tomorrow. We can be over the Olympus Badlands by early afternoon. They turned northwest.

Badlands, he thought. It was one of the great mountains of the Solar System when he was last here.

A river meandered through the long low depression still known as Valles Marineris, and interestingly, several bends had been isolated, cut off by changes in the river course. They camped that night on the river shores. Ingrid caught a huge catfish and they dined well. Still recovering his reserves, Tohn slept soundly and dreamed that he was so dead to the world that Ingrid couldn't even shake him awake.

It was actually just after sunrise the following day when they approached the old mountain, having stopped on impulse at the museum of Port Lowell. The circular outline of the badlands betrayed the location of the ancient shield, and a cluster of impressive hard basaltic towers betrayed the location of the old crater. They were shrouded in mist rising from the pools of water which had collected in hollows between the old plugs.

"Don't touch the water," Ingrid warned him after they landed near the base of a ten thousand meter monolithic plug of fossil lava.

Then it hit him. The water wasn't misting, it was steaming.

"It's active! But how?"

Her laughter rung in chains.

"There's still a small planet's worth of radioactive decay going on inside Mars, and will be for billions of years to come. It has to come out somewhere. And we've suddenly changed the hydrostatic balance with so much erosion. The land under the old mountain is lifting again, some places a centimeter a year. It's cracking and rubbing against itself. All sorts of friction. Didn't you feel the quake last night?" She pressed herself to him.

The ten thousand meter tower next to him was considerably taller than broad. He looked at both it and her apprehensively.

"I've changed myself, yes. A little way back to what we were before. I think there are too few real people in this universe now, don't you?"

"Well, yes." That was his philosophy, his reason for continuing in the face of six million years of repetition. "But I'm not sure what the point is anymore." He thought of Kairl.

"The point! Look around you! Does there have to be a point to this? It's wonderful. Don't tell me it's not — I saw that look in your eye, at the eclipse, at the steam vents. Tohn, we are the first people to live long enough to see the long pulse of nature. We can see a species evolve toward sentience. We can see the land boil and flow. Change. Rebirth. You can watch the majesty of it unfold and it fills you, or you die.

"They're dead now, or gone, those who weren't filled by it. We're the new race by virtue of surviving." Ingrid laughed. "We can watch the Solar System as the sun grows and the planets move out, we can guide new species to sapience, and we can see the stars swirl and dance in the Milky Way. I think we should populate this world again, with people like us. Let's start, right now."

Something she was doing, something she was sending out, infecting him with, or body language perhaps, maybe smell, was making him feel things he hadn't felt for ages. Her hands were on him, removing his clothing. He didn't mind. He laughed, kissed her, and released the front of her jumpsuit. Unnecessary things fell like dry leaves at their feet as they embraced among the now stirring bones of ancient Olympus Mons.

"It's a spring morning and I can love you like no one has loved for millions of years," she told him when they rested. "We aren't old; the stars are old. We're young. We are ten million years young and it's all just beginning." The planet shuddered in agreement, and some rocks fell in the distance. He looked up.

AFTERWORD — MORNING ON MARS

THIS STORY WAS INSPIRED by a visit to Lassen National Park in northern California, where I learned, among other things, that volcanic mountains can be worn down by rain in wind in a few million years. Of course, they can also be blasted away in a few tenths of a second by an eruption or an asteroid impact. The surfaces of some planets change faster than others, but almost everything, on the geological or astronomical scale of time, is ephemeral — nature's sidewalk paintings, if you like.

I look at the question of whether we should or shouldn't terraform Mars from that perspective. And unless I have the forward march of cybernetic and biological technology entirely wrong, it is the perspective that our descendants may be taking in not too many generations. It is, ultimately, a question of esthetics; Mars is not Antarctica; it is not part of the fragile ecosystem in which people live, it is not subject to multiple territorial claims, the melting of its icecaps would not drown a hundred legendary human cities. The only harm to be done by terraforming Mars is the harm to the egos and esthetic senses of people who would not have anything done period. In the grander scheme of things, it is like building sand castles.

Mars may even terraform itself every now and then. There are times when its orbital eccentricity and the phasing of its seasons may conspire to make it much warmer there ("much" in this context is but a few Kelvins, but that is said to be enough), warm enough to evaporate the carbon dioxide and increase the atmospheric pressure to the point where liquid water can exist.

Our descendants will do a somewhat more thorough job of this ourselves, when they get around to it. More on that later.

"Morning on Mars" is one of the shortest stories I have ever sold, but also takes one of the farthest look into the future. In it, technology has generally advanced to physical limits and there are an overwhelming number of possibilities for existence, a few of which are hinted at. One of those options is conservative; some people may choose to remain as recognizably human beings, albeit much perfected beings, though with many of our infirmities of mind and body abolished. Another will be the ability to "upload" one's mind to a suitable cybernetic platform at will. The "Mind of Mars" is such a platform, which I have located in the moons of Mars.

I mention physical limits. Knowledge, unfortunately, must advance at the expense of possibilities — a thousand theories die for every one that survives its tests against the universe. We do not know everything, of course. But we do know a fair amount, and among those things is that the speed of light always measures the same regardless of how fast one is moving with respect to the source of the light. The logical consequence of this is that the structure of time, order and consequence are such that, unless everything is rigged in advance, one cannot reach a given destination sooner than a photon of light racing through a vacuum, without also traveling through time and, inevitably, creating a situation where two mutually exclusive states of being would have to exist at the same time — a fairly common definition of "impossible."

Thus, it takes Tohn a full 2 million years to journey to the great galaxy in Andromeda and two million years back. Thus, the Mind of Mars must be physically close to Mars to interact with Martians. I freely admit the alternative of a predestined universe would resolve temporal paradoxes and, as yet, there is no proof that time travel cannot be done and that the universe is thus not predestined. I do not know if such a proof is even possible. Think about it; what would one accept as "proof?" But after a lot of consideration, I've decided not to go that route. It may be a naive view, but to me the universe looks profoundly unpredestined and highly contingent with lots of random input at the quantum level. This suits me just fine because I would rather think that our choices have real contingent consequences. Anyway, writers must make choices and I have chosen to write about a future which is intended to be contingent and consistent with what we know of physical law.

In "Morning on Mars" the sand castle that human beings have built is beginning to wash away. Without plate tectonics, eventually the mountains will wash away and the new oceans will silt up. Perhaps they will be dredged. With sufficiently advanced technology, Mars could be maintained in whatever state people wish it to be. But I think that eventually, people will find it more interesting to watch it change.

Also, in five billion years or so, the Sun will start burning helium and grow into a "red giant" star — far brighter in the infrared than in visible light-that will likely consume anything that remains in Earth's orbit. But, perhaps, it will only give Mars a good toasting.

My somewhat tongue-in-cheek alien archeologists have found evidence of three civilizations in those five billion years, but, at a rate of some ten to twenty million years per civilization, it could easily be three hundred. Such numbers make one shiver, but shivers are not a constraint.

Whatever. After consuming its innermost children and blasting away its outermost layers, the sun will contract, grow increasingly dense, and become a "white dwarf." The remaining planets orbits will expand due to the sun's loss of mass. Along the way, for a period of time much shorter than Tohn's lifespan but much longer than all of human history to date, the sun will be at the right luminosity for there to be, once again, life on Mars.

A WORLD TO TAKE

ALTHOR HAD MUD on his tentacles. His hive daughters had built a vast spinning wheel near the orbit of one of the planet's five glicking-fruit-shaped satellites, all carefully arranged in stable resonance orbits. Well, of course, they wouldn't be there if they weren't in stable resonances, Eldest Daughter would tell him, so that doesn't prove anything.

Still Althor suspected.

The wheel spun with just the right speed to duplicate the gravity of Althor's home world, and its holds had been filled with planet stuff, bodily lifted to where it could be studied in bare tentacles and without mechanical aids for walking. Althor's people came from a world much like the largest satellite of the third planet — the gas giant with the rings — and it was that world which had attracted their attention. But, it had proved to have an atmosphere only a tenth as deep as that of Althor's home world, and had only briefly been warm enough to provide a suitable environment.

Althor had mud on his tentacles, literally and figuratively. Eldest Daughter had deliberately postponed her sex change to stay with him, rather than to mate and lead her own hive to the stars. And now, this.

There was enough mass in this overcooked cinder below them to make five to ten planets the size of Althor's world. Their machines could do the job in a few hundred revolutions. But Eldest Daughter was aghast at the notion.

"We have three billion revolutions of civilization to explore! Who knows what may have gone on here? Aren't you curious? Look at that thing!"

Althor held a box, salvaged from what had clearly been a flying machine of what they'd began to call the "first civilization" from the oldest layers of silt east of the main continent. The bulk of the machine was being disencased from what muck becomes if sat on for four billion revolutions. The rock was being washed off to his right by high-pressure jets wielded with microscope precision by their robots — and it was mud once again.

"A power source," he said at length. "From the size of the conduits in and out, it clearly wasn't a computer, even a primitive one. But it seems to be solid state, and rather smaller than I would have expected, to power something that could fly in the gravity below."

"It's the third one we've found. Hive-Father, they were filled with Carbon-60."

"Pleatorballs?"

"Galaxies and galaxies of them all arranged in neat little rows. Two-thirds of the mass of this thing is pleatorballs. But there's no evidence of any kind of chemistry. Do you know what it is?"

Althor had to admit he didn't, and that was the figurative mud on his tentacles. "It's a mystery to me."

"Yes! A mystery! This isn't just any world, Hive-Father. Layer upon layer of artifacts — it must have been continuously inhabited until its sun turned — but maintained in a more or less natural state. A park world, mostly."

Sun turned... The solution reached Althor immediately. It had to be right.

"Hive-Daughter, check those pleatorballs very carefully, for I suspect that in each is an impurity which gives them a magnetic moment. They are flywheels, and in their frame would be the means to spin them up and pull the energy from their spin. Mystery solved."

Her tentacles drooped.

"Ahem... But, Eldest Daughter, your point is well taken. Most planets are rapidly overbuilt by their first civilizations, until they learn better. The philosophy that prevailed here would be interesting: be assured of as much time as you need. We can make worlds of other things."

THE DAY OF THEIR COMING

THEY SAY YOU ALWAYS remember just where you were when great events happen, and I certainly remember this one. On the morning of the twenty-third of Taurus, I was wandering alone along the shore of the Chryse Sea, near the creek that cut through the bluff below our family home, when the universe changed.

The woodpeckers woke me, tapping their way into my dreams, forcing me to admit the night was gone and I had perhaps a few precious minutes left to slip out and watch the sunrise before Mom and Dad woke and started to throw chores around. It was clear and cool, about twenty-two Celsius or so, which, I reflected, was about as warm as it *ever* got on old Mars. So I put on a pair of shorts and a sweatshirt and slipped out the screen door and headed barefoot down the sandy path past the guesthouse over the reddish dunes toward the sea.

The Ritters were sleeping in the guesthouse, with their daughter Krin. Krin and I had grown up next door to each other, and we had been just getting to know each other again at that age when people start becoming people when Dad had gotten a raise and we'd moved to a bigger house in another neighborhood. She was a little bigger than me in the year before we left, so when we played games, she was the princess of Mars, I was her slave, and I had to do what she said. Anything at all. Like taking the trash out. That move had been my first heartbreak; our families kept in touch, but in an adult world, kids' friendships are expendable. Krin and I saw each other long enough to say hello maybe every year or so when the families got together.

The early morning was my silent, clean, private, magic time. Martian shortwing daygulls were soaring, cawing, looking for shellfish on the receding tide. The sun poked up over the woods on the eastern shore of the bay, a spot of brilliant yellow. I wished Krin was with me. She liked the sun; we'd gone swimming and sunbathing together every year since my family built the place.

Half-daydreaming, I was looking at a big frog, who was thinking he was invisible, sitting among the stones in the creek which flowed into the bay, now glittering gold with sunrise, when Mom called out down the hill in her opera-singing voice to say that an alien starship had arrived.

Mom wouldn't kid about something like that, so I ran up to the house as fast as I could.

When I got there, Mrs. Ritter was making breakfast for us, while Dad, Dr. Ritter, and Krin had their eyes glued to a long-range view of the starship displayed on the living room viewscreen, listening as Elin Komoto and a host of other newsreaders tried to explain how the alien spacecraft had suddenly shown up in the Martian orbital traffic pattern and asked for port clearance in passable English.

The alien starship was different than anything of ours — a single large sphere rather than a ring of spheres. I looked for Mom, but she was already on the phone with some of her engineering friends in the study. I sat next to Krin, close enough to touch, but she didn't seem to notice — with that to look at, I didn't wonder. My thoughts, however, kept bouncing between her and the starship.

It was only in the last couple years that we'd become good friends again; Krin had put away chasing frogs and salamanders for big girl things much earlier than I had been ready for. At four, her hair had turned from gold to brown, she was taller than I was, and she didn't want much to do with me. By the time we were five, I was reading voraciously, and had some grown-up things to talk about, but we didn't see each other that year.

I started having fantasies about her when I was six, the year we built this country house. Dad wanted to get back to the land; Viking City had been getting too crowded for him. The Ritters had visited for a day that year, and I had shown Earth, Venus, and mighty Jove to

Krin on that special summer evening. Then, the following year, we'd actually held hands, briefly.

So when the Ritters arrived at the "farm," I was already full of anticipation. Krin was only a month short of her eighth Martian birthday, and we were still about the same height. Her hair was a sun-lightened reddish brown, cut self-confidently and boyishly short. We were both bookworms now, and instant buddies again. But she shattered my romantic dreams by announcing that she now had a very serious boyfriend, a New Reformationist named Ed Kelso, back at Marsport prep, so that whatever we did was just for old times and not serious.

She wore a ring with a fish symbol, but she wasn't married *yet*, and so I resolved to show her a better alternative without being too pushy. I hoped that Ed Kelso wasn't the jealous type.

"When will we see the Aliens?" Krin asked.

Dr. Ritter frowned. He was a big man with short white hair, and when he frowned, it looked serious. "We should have pictures by now. I don't understand why not."

"I wonder how the starship works," I added. "A pusher beam would hit it straight on and fry the crew — Dad, do you think they have some other kind of drive?"

"Too early to tell. They've got Ellie working on it already." He nodded toward Mom.

Dr. Ritter was drafted too. He took his first call in the kitchen because Mom had the study tied up. Later on, the people to whom he was talking became the Contact Committee, but just then everyone was scrambling. The government had asked the starship to hold off Phobos, away from the congestion of the port of Deimos, and equally far away from public and academic scrutiny.

We spent the rest of the early morning laughing at the media instant analysis people getting all sorts of technical stuff wrong by trying to oversimplify, or just by being scientifically over their heads. Komoto did the best, as I remember, just sticking to what, when, and where. Once, she started to read something about the aliens coming twenty-five parsecs in three and a half years, then stopped, saying: "Well, *that* has nothing to do with reality," and quickly moved on to something else.

Dad explained; "It should have been about three and a half parsecs in twenty-five years. If they'd use light years instead of parsecs, no one would get confused. Also, the aliens didn't come from Cor Caroli, but from a pair of red dwarf stars much closer, and they were only visiting *there*. But this ship came from the direction of Cor Caroli, and, reasonably enough, identified itself as originating from that direction." He grimaced. "They learned English on the way in, and fancied they could speak it. Those government flacks will have everyone calling them Korkol for years."

It didn't help that the New Reformationists were floating rumors that it was all a hoax and whining about balanced reporting. This sort of obfuscation should have been a warning, but my mind was elsewhere. With the Ritters planning to leave tomorrow, I didn't have much time left with Krin, and I began to resent the aliens for monopolizing what little there was left. So, when we realized they'd just been saying the same thing over and over again for the last half hour, I asked Krin out for a swim.

She laughed. "Okay. I'm bored and it's hot. Just don't tell Ed."

We excused ourselves and headed for the lake, really just a very wide section of the creek that flowed into the sea. I dropped my shorts on the towels and waded in. She followed, still wearing her long white New Reformationist shirt.

"Wait a minute," I protested. "Nobody swims with their clothes on!"

"The New Reformationists do. Ed says nobody can see a woman's body except the man who owns her."

"Krin, I've already seen your body, every time you've been out here. Besides, that thing will get all wet. Your mom and my mom don't wear anything when they swim and nothing's ever happened to them because of it. Not that you look like Mom yet."

She stuck her tongue out at me. "Wait until Ed and I start having babies." Then she looked serious for a moment. "I've got to get used to a lot of new ideas. But, you're right. It's silly." She dropped the shirt on the pile of towels and clothes. "I'll beat you across the lake!"

A hundred yards across the lake was a beach. She beat me there easily: she'd been on the academy swim team until she'd met Ed. We lay out on the sand and talked.

"Just think," Krin said. "We're completely out of sight of anything artificial: just the sand, the sky, the water, and us!"

Of course, the sand and water and air and sky were all there by courtesy of planetary engineering, but I didn't want to break her mood so I gave her an noncommittal grunt. I suppose this was one case where what one felt was more important than reality.

"I can't talk like this with Ed. They have guy's stuff here and women's stuff there — all segregated. I guess I'll just have to get used to it."

I just couldn't see Krin as a New Reformationist.

The news people had thought they'd have pictures of the aliens by noon, so we swam back to the other shore, wrapped towels around our waists, and carrying our clothes, made our way back through the dunes and trees. When we got to the house the warm breeze from the Tharsis high desert had us pretty dry and he news coverage was still on. But it put out even less information than before.

Komoto was interviewing a New Reformationist bishop who was pointing out that nobody had actually *seen* an alien yet, that no one had actually seen the ship come from outside the solar system, and that the whole thing could have been faked. Ten years later, of course, they're sending missions to Tau Ceti and saying this was all part of the great plan foretold in New Reformation scripture. But that day, this bozo was trying to deny the whole thing and Krin didn't look happy at

all listening to him. I caught Dr. Ritter looking at her very thoughtful-
ly.

There were no pictures of aliens yet. Komoto was reporting that
the authorities said there were "delays in working out the digital
interface" between the starship and the planetary communications net
with a skeptical edge to her voice when the house interrupted to tell
Mom that the local news people wanted to set up an interview about
the alien propulsion system. She told it that she didn't know anything
about the particulars yet, but to tell them she would be happy to talk
on the general subject.

Frustrated with the news pabulum, Krin and I went to my room to
look for some real background. I dug out a cyberbook and some data
wands, loaded one on spacecraft, and flopped down on the rug. I
called up a diagram of the solar system navigation aids to show how
the aliens had surprised everyone by coming in from far below the
plane of the planets' orbits. All the radar and optics were concentrated
on the ecliptic, where all the traffic was. Krin's arm pressed against
mine and it was hard to keep my mind on things.

Next, I loaded a biology stick and went right to the speculative
stuff at the end where the authors were guessing about what aliens
would be like.

"I think I have to read the first part to understand this," Krin
sighed. "What's convergent evolution?"

"That's the idea that similar environmental problems evolve similar solutions. Like kangaroos and deer, or bats and owls. Some people
think it applies to cultural development, too, and aliens will be a lot
like us. Others say no, they'll be too weird to even talk to."

"If they're *that* weird," Krin asked, "why would they want to talk to
us, or even visit us?"

"Good question. Uh, I just remembered I've got to recycle the fax
paper." Mom used a lot of hard copy in her engineering business; it
was a lot less expensive than having dozens of cyberbooks for thing
she wanted to have in front of her all the time. One of my chores was
to gather up all the used paper and stick it in the recycler to be laser
bleached and used again.

I got a sharp look from Mom as I put a stack in the almost-empty
hopper just in time. Mom had ordered all sorts of stuff about magnetic sails and neutral particle beam-focusing, and it came about as fast

as I could keep the hopper full. She had diagrams pasted up all over the walls of the study. In fact, it was clear that we were going to need more paper, so we started organizing a trip into town.

Then, in the stuff they sent Mom, we got our first look at the Korkol. A diagram of a Korkol spacesuit had somehow slipped through. In fact, that was how we realized that data were definitely being censored. Dad was phlegmatic as usual, but Mom and Dr. Ritter were furious.

One look at Mom's back-channel stuff and it was obvious why the Korkol came to Mars rather than Earth; we've got a third the gravity and almost twice the atmospheric pressure. If you're a Korkol, that makes it a lot easier to fly. To me, they looked a bit like a cross between a frog and a crow, but that makes them sound ugly. They weren't. They looked *right*.

I went to get Krin to show her, and asked her if she wanted to go to Viking City for paper and blank data rods with us. She didn't answer right away, playing with the fish ring on her hand. "I probably should," she finally said, sighed, gave me a little hug, and kissed my cheek. "I've got to get some stuff and talk to Dad." My heart was beating so loud from the kiss that I was sure that everyone in the house could hear it, but I held together, somehow.

Meanwhile, Mom had started the interview using the main screen in the living room instead of the study, because the background in the study was too messy. She'd even put on a businesslike jump suit. Krin and I walked right behind her, still in our beach towels, not realizing we were live across the whole planet; Mom had put the comm unit on the coffee table to get her living room view in the background. Dad almost laughed out loud in the middle of Mom's interview, but held himself together and motioned us to the side, out of the field of view.

We stopped to listen to the interview.

The news people were trying to get Mom to say that the Korkol had some dangerous new sort of physics. Mom wasn't sure of that and wouldn't give them a supporting quote. It was all very polite, but afterward, when we saw the edited broadcast, it looked like Mom was warning about alien technology, too. She wasn't amused, and went to make some calls.

Krin and her father went to the guest house and I went out to get the buzzer ready, jealous again of the time away from Krin. I hooked up the power line to the spinner and torqued up my buckyballs. A fluorinated buckyball spinning at a hundred teraradians per second packs five times as much energy as rocket fuel in one-tenth the volume — you can fly around Mars all day on that.

But if people like the New Reformationists had been in charge three centuries back when that was discovered, well, it wouldn't have been discovered. At least that's how I saw it. I felt rotten seeing Krin go over to them. She was too smart. But there was nothing I could do. Zero. She'd made up her mind and I'd just have to stop dreaming about her. Sure.

Dr. Ritter and Krin came out, bags packed, while I was doing a preflight fan check. I hadn't realized that Krin was leaving too, and that in the tender moment in the room, she'd been saying goodbye. She was back in her New Reformation shirt, now. I just paid very close attention to the spinner and the inspection plates. Dad says I'm fussy, but my license is less than a year old.

While I monitored the spin-up, Dr. Ritter explained that there was a problem with the New Reformation diocese brass holding back information about the aliens, and he was going to try to help negotiate. Krin's old man has a gift for understatement; the Church of the New Reformation was pulling out all the political power stops to keep a lid on things. It seemed that on top of the inconvenience of their existence, the aliens' religion was founded on natural law, and had no place in it for supernatural beings.

"Just because they're aliens doesn't make them right," Krin protested. "Is that all?"

"Their life cycle is patently obscene, by New Reformation standards," he said with an ironic grin. "That isn't surprising, though; by those same standards, so is ours."

Krin didn't like this comment very much, and I could sense things weren't going well. I hoped.

I asked if they'd be coming back again next summer, and that's when I found out that in the New Reformation you were expected to marry early and start having babies, right through school.

"That's too soon!" I heard myself say.

Dr. Ritter grimaced. "Perhaps, but it makes economic sense, given the New Reformations extended family support system and their deliberately limited requirements for formal education," he admitted.

"Schoolwork isn't easy, but, really, most of it can be done at home. By the time the young parents are ready to be economically independent, the first kids are old enough to babysit the youngest ones."

I was surprised to hear him say anything nice about the New Reformation, but as a sociologist, I guess he had to be objective. Krin wasn't. She was enthusiastic.

"We'll have a couple of kids, our own house, and our own land when most kids are still wrapped up in football and beer busts," Krin claimed. "It's a more natural, organic lifestyle. I'll be free of all the stresses of conforming to the artificial needs of modern civilization."

"The New Reformation lifestyle has stresses of its own," her father warned, "particularly in the conformity area. What's the purpose of living the way they do, just repeating the same cycle, generation after generation? Where are they going?"

"They're content just to follow God's plan," she countered. "It's the process that counts, and it feels right to me." It was clear they'd had this argument before, and neither gave in.

What, I thought as I topped off the charge, was wrong with *me*? I'd be perfectly willing to make babies with Krin, if that's what she wanted. I was sure my folks would be happy to put us up for a while; we could do all the farming you could ever want to do on our land, and had the robots to do it with. She wouldn't have to pretend to swallow any of the New Reformationist garbage, like the stuff that bishop-whoever was putting out about the aliens (I found out later that the Bishop's name was Kelso, too). But Krin was smart, determined, and way over my head, so, as usual, I said nothing.

The tone indicating full charge sounded so I stowed the spinner and its leads, and pronounced us ready. We got in the buzzer and took off. I had it do a pass over our place before heading to the Viking City shuttle port. Dad and Mrs. Ritter waved. Mom was busy. I had the buzzer record everything, so I could send Krin the cube. It's pretty impressive: the domed house on the bluff overlooking both the lake and the bay at the point of a green wedge of irrigated fields and forest stretching almost twenty kilometers north, to the Shalbatana valley.

Viking City was sited a couple of hundred kilometers up the Shalbatana back before anyone was sure about where the Chryse Sea shoreline would stabilize. It was almost a kilometer higher than we were; they had wanted to be sure it would stay high and dry. Also, it was a little cooler up there, though not much. Altitude makes a lot more difference on a high-gravity planet like Earth.

I took us down to the Shalbatana through the red fluted gorge of LeRenard River. That's us, the LeRenards. When you're in at the ground floor, like great-grandfather, your name gets on things. Our family goes back to the old Mars third colony ship, before there was any New Reformation and "Saint" Thomas Solacus was still a mechanic. Then I turned west, up river, and we watched the rapids and forests go by below.

We listened for news of the aliens, but heard nothing new. Dr. Ritter voiced his concerns.

"Some New Reformationists want the Korkol to go away so they can pretend that the whole thing was a hoax. They have the votes to influence politics to the extent that information about the aliens is being voluntarily censored at the bishops' request, to give them time to invent a new party line."

Krin thought that this was just a fringe element. She was sure Ed and his folks weren't like that at all. Yes, they had all the romantic reserve, quaint manners, and politeness of their sect's reputation; but they used robots too, and Ed was getting a Marsport prep education. She said she could believe in God in a Deist, metaphysical way, just ignore their theology, and get along fine.

Dr. Ritter disagreed. He thought there were a lot of people who like to be told what to think, and that the New Reformationists were breeding and training people like that as fast as they could.

Time goes quickly when you're discussing subjects like that. Before I knew it, or could figure out how to say goodbye, the buzzer linked and flowed into the traffic pattern at West Viking City Field. As we came down, Krin recognized Ed and a couple of his friends on the fringe of the grass, waiting for us, at least they were the only ones wearing New Reformation shirts in the thirty-five Celsius midday heat. He was a big redhead, about twenty-five or so, a couple of meters tall, and looked used to using his hands. I was pretty sure I didn't want to find out if he was the jealous type or not.

Krin was surprised and excited that Ed was there, and she jumped out of the buzzer as soon as the fans stopped and the doors unlocked. No goodbyes. Dr. Ritter looked at me and shrugged; I guess what I was feeling was pretty obvious to everybody but Krin. She ran up to

Ed, arms open and a look of unmitigated joy on her face. He didn't react to her until she was right up to him.

And then, with a powerful blow from the back of his hand to her face, he knocked her flat to the ground. Dr. Ritter was out of the buzzer pretty fast, for an old guy, but I got there first and jumped on Ed Kelso, pulling him to the ground. Something very hard hit the back of my head.

That was the last thing I remember until waking up on a cot in the Viking City jail. Well, they called it a public safety facility, but I couldn't walk out. Dad had to come to get me. He said Krin had pleaded with Ed and his family not to press charges against her father and me, and she left with them on that condition, bruised and sobbing.

Dr. Ritter wasn't in much better shape than I was, but he'd gone on up the tethertube to Deimos despite his injuries an hour ago. He said he was motivated do whatever he could to make the New Reformationists uncomfortable. When we got home, Mom was tight-lipped and Mrs. Ritter was all over me, crying. I almost wished I'd stayed in jail, I was so embarrassed.

When everyone settled down, they told me what happened. When Krin and I had walked through Mom's interview, all Mars had seen us before the New Reformation censors realized that Krin was a girl. Ed Kelso had gone ballistic because she hadn't kept covered up like he told her to.

That was my fault, only Mrs. Ritter didn't seem to blame me at all. She was just very unhappy and very concerned. We couldn't even contact Krin by phone.

Mom wasn't mad at me either, but she was as angry as I've ever seen her about a lot of other things. When she gets that look, *something* usually happens. Dad was in his "Ellie, let's think this out before we do anything stupid" mode.

The public news had dried up to hourly bulletins. We were getting one to the effect that there was nothing new about the "alleged" alien spacecraft when Dr. Ritter called from Deimos. It seemed that the New Reformation bishops had just about persuaded the Korkol that their presence would be very unsettling to the established social order, and that the civilized thing to do would be to withdraw.

"The aliens aren't idiots," he fumed. "They waited for years in the inner comet belt, learning our language and analyzing. But we can't get through to them. Our Martian Planetary President isn't part of the New Reformation, but he needs their votes in a close contest, and he's caved in. Everything has to go through a cultural affairs bureaucrat sympathetic to the New Reformation, and it's apparent that the only thing that got out to the president and the Korkol was stuff that tended to support the New Reformation culture shock ideology. I've got to get back now, Ellie, maybe you can get through this log jam." We said goodbye and he signed off.

"Mom," I said. "Why don't we just talk to the aliens directly, ourselves."

"The contact committee won't put us through. They're censoring everything."

"We've got our own dish. Maybe the aliens have already figured out our communications system. That's what we'd do if we came into an inhabited solar system."

"Well, yes. But the starship's at Phobos."

"I can rig up a sight, and steer the antenna manually as Phobos goes by."

Mom looked at me for a long while. "We could get into trouble, even if it works. But I think I'm willing to risk it. How about you?" She looked at Dad. He shut his eyes for a little, then nodded without saying anything. The Viking county government could take everything that my family had accumulated in four generations away from us, if it got mad enough. And it was dominated by New Reformationists. Dad was literally betting the farm with that nod, though I didn't realize much of this until I was a lot older.

"You'd better go to it. Phobos is already past zenith."

I grabbed the sonodrill, liquid clamp, a solar cell with a test light, a multi-wrench, and some molding, then headed for the roof. I drilled a small hole in the back of the dish and used the liquid clamp to glue a stick onto the subreflector support at about the same azimuth as the hole. I glued the solar cell to the subreflector and ran the test bulb wires to the back of the dish. After releasing the azimuth and elevation lock bolts, I manually swung it over toward the setting sun.

The dish is white and concentrates sunlight just like microwaves, though not as efficiently. The solar cell would be at maximum output when the dish's rough image of the sun fell on the center of the subreflector, which would happen when the antenna was pointed at the sun, so I moved the dish around until I got a maximum, then peeked through the hole I'd drilled to see where the sun was along the stick. I put a hole in the piece of wood there, then double checked to make sure the holes lined up on the sun while the solar cell output was maximum. They did, close enough. I beat the sunset by about five minutes.

I knocked on the skylight and gave Dad a thumbs up to let him know I was ready. Then I sighted the antenna on Phobos, and started tracking. Dad came out to say that we'd established contact and stayed to spell me for a while. We alternated for almost half an hour, until Phobos set.

When we got back in, Mom told us that she had gotten through to the Chief Engineer of the Korkol starship. They'd all learned passable English during their trip in from the outskirts of the solar system, and when the Korkol engineers found out about the problems Mom was having with censorship, they had been very cooperative.

"We're learning a lot from each other," she said, with a smile. "They're getting a little tired of the politics, too, and they're going to move up to Deimos, right in the face of church objections."

Good for them, I thought, preoccupied with misery now that the task was over. If the Korkol hadn't come, we'd never have made the trip to Marsport, and Krin would still be here. I went outside to walk some of the blues away. Just that morning, my arms and head didn't ache, there were no aliens, and I had gone swimming with Krin.

I found Mrs. Ritter out there, on the grass at the edge of the bluff overlooking the sea, her straight golden hair streaming down her back to those baggy, pockety walking shorts she always wore. She was staring at the still-sunlit line of the Demos-Tharsis tethertube just over the horizon. At the end was a point of light, Deimos, and another, fainter one moving toward it. The starship, already? Her husband was up there now, with the contact committee.

She greeted me with a smile, and motioned for me to sit next to her. "The tube curves up like that, to miss Phobos, I know," she waved her arms at the tethertube. "But you'd think the end would have to be at the equator. How can it do that?"

I could answer that one, pulling myself out of self-pity for a bit. "Imagine yourself at the north pole. Okay?" She nodded. "Now, you've got a bucket with a very long rope. Swing it around your head so it doesn't hit the ice." She laughed and pretended to shiver.

"Now, just keep letting the rope out."

"Oh! I think I understand now." She paused, reflecting, then added, "There's a way around every impossible-seeming thing if you think carefully enough, isn't there?

"Well, sometimes," I answered.

"Your mother is so good at that, and I can see she's taught you very well."

Maybe it was because she was so unthreatening, so simple in the best sense of the word, that I could tell her what I couldn't say to Krin, to Dad, to Dr. Ritter and certainly not to Mom.

"Uh, Mrs. Ritter, I think I love Krin," I blurted. "I don't know what to do about it. Looks hopeless."

She just put an arm around me and held me as we sat there while the shadow of Mars crept up the shining strand of the tethertube and eclipsed both the moon and the starship.

Then I thought of something I could do. It wouldn't get Krin back, but at least it would hurt the New Reformationists and maybe it would help Dr. Ritter. I had left the buzzer's cameras on when we landed at Viking City; everything that had happened that noon had been recorded. If all Mars and the Aliens could see what had happened...

I told Mrs. Ritter, and her eyes lit up. "I've got an old boyfriend in the news department of one of the independent commercial networks. Maybe he could use a scoop." We got busy.

The news people put it all together: Mom's interview, the fight at the landing field, the phony charges, and Krin trading her own freedom for her father's and mine. They didn't have to say anything about New Reformationist intolerance and censorship: they just showed it, along with our faxes of the Korkol. The public network news people stuck their necks out and ran the story too.

What a commotion that caused! Preempted programs, angry editorials, clogged comm channels, and my family right in the middle of it. Mars could still be outraged, and in the ensuing reaction the president quickly dropped the effort to appease the New Reformation bishops with censorship.

Dr. Ritter called from Deimos; the Aliens had arrived and all efforts to manage the contact on the basis of culture shock had been dropped: what was, was. People would just have to adapt. He asked if we'd mind playing host to some colleagues. Mom was enthusiastic, despite how late it was getting, and Dad went to pick him up at Viking City field two hours later.

Getting the true, confirmed story, the Home Planet reacted too. A fleet of politicians, bureaucrats, and newships set out from Earth, despite its unfavorable orbital position.

The New Reformationists beat the drums of technophobia, but by then Mom was ready with a full explanation of the Korkol propulsion system: their pusher beams weren't as narrow as ours so they simply used end shielding and a bigger target field. There was another part of their starship which they hadn't brought into the inner solar system with them; their magnetic sail, a thin gossamer spider web of superconducting cables many kilometers across, which was still orbiting in the inner comet belt. No warp drive or anything like that.

Their slowdown system was ingenious, however. They put mirrors at the nodes of the magsail, forming an array which could focus a high-powered laser across several astronomical units. They used that setup to vaporize and ionize bits of comet which lay in their path, and run into the resulting ionized gas with the magsail, which acts like a parachute.

Diverting slightly from comet to comet, they'd bumped along through the Oort belt to a stop well outside Eris' orbit. No magic, no new physics, not even any really new technological capabilities; just superlatively clever application. Mom was in seventh heaven — seeming more happy than the situation warranted, at least from my perspective.

I felt she was acting as if Krin didn't matter, but all I could think of was Krin, who I knew loved freedom, being ordered around, bred, and beaten in some New Reformationist hellhole. And, yes, I was a little jealous about the breeding part.

Late that night, Dad and Dr. Ritter arrived alone. I asked about his guests, and he said they had to pick someone up in the Valles and would be by a little latter. Mom looked tense.

Cold currents from the Boreal Ocean well up just beyond our bay, bringing cool breezes after midnight off the Chryse Sea. We all went outside to the lanai as the air finally cooled off and nightgulls coasted overhead, crying as if they too felt my loss. We leaned on the rail and gazed at the Southern Cross floating over the still bay, wondering who besides the Korkol might be out there.

"Well, there will be a lot of fish," Dad remarked, his thoughts always nearer to home. "There's talk of allowing fishing on the bay in a couple of years. We could be running tour boats or fishing boats from here." He had to raise his voice over the sound of the nightgulls' flapping wings.

That seemed strange. Nightgulls don't flap much; they soar. I looked up.

He appeared suddenly, coming out of the star-studded black, invisible until some stray light from inside the house caught him — a large winged being holding some sort of weapon in his hands. He swooped down from overhead and lit on the rail in front of mother so that his head would be even with hers. She greeted him as a friend, relieved, but not at all surprised by the Korkol Chief Engineer's visit. I just stood there, awe-struck.

But the flapping noises continued, and I looked around in surprise. Then, from the front of the lanai, I saw four more Korkol carrying something suspended on a sling between them. They came lower and on their sling I could see a person wearing a tattered long white robe, a black eye, and a big grin. As they set her gently down on the lanai, everyone called Krin's name. But she rushed to *me*. Mom grinned and winked. I should have known.

I think the Korkol said something to Mom about civilized beings having to stick together, but I didn't catch it all; I was much too busy with Krin.

And so I missed the beginnings of the compact which has saved, in my judgment at least, part of humanity from this growing new dark age.

♂ ♂ ♂

In later years, we would write at length (Length? Nowadays they call us the Martian Durants!) about my planet's history and the convergent cultural evolution of spacefaring cultures. But, even then, it was pretty clear to me that our free-thinking families had more in common with the free-flying Korkol star travelers than we would ever have with the New Reformationists. A division of sorts is happening, one that has less to do with biological nature than with intellectual heritage and the mindset needed to prosper in a space-faring life. Some will be able to go on, some will not.

The Korkol stayed with us that night, and for several nights thereafter, talking with Mom and Dr. Ritter. When they took a break, Krin and I would show them where they could find fish, and they delighted in stooping down from the sky and catching the fish in their feet. The Korkol would talk to each other in a high-pitched, burbly sort of sound, and they always let the fish go.

Krin and I were married the next year, thanks in ironical part to an early marriage law the New Reformationists managed to push through. We were not economically independent, but with the loving support of both families, we continued our lives and grew together. We built a small house on the shores of the Chryse Sea with our own hands and helped supplement my writing income by running Father's tourist boats around the bay.

Our children's children live in that house now. When Father passed on, we moved up to the old residence. There, on the warm tropical nights of the Chryse seashore, we can take our canes, walk out on the lanai, and hold hands as we look up to the stars. There, on the very spot it happened so many years ago, we can remember that magical night when my princess was borne down to me from the sky on the wings of angels.

AFTERWORD — THE DAY OF THEIR COMING

HOPEFULLY, IT TOOK LESS TIME for the title to remind you of Poul Anderson's "The Day of Their Return" than it did me, at least consciously. But I wouldn't change it, for in addition to conjuring thoughts of flying sophants, I hope it reminds one of another Anderson theme, that of aliens and humans in a similar line of work having more in common with each other than perhaps others of their own species.

An oft-heard criticism of science fiction these days is that the aliens aren't alien enough. When it comes to the makeup of Star Trek actors, well, yes, I wouldn't begrudge a chuckle or two. But there is a larger issue with not so much the physical form, but with how aliens behave and are motivated relative to the range of human behavior.

Let us first consider the patterns of motivation that we have in common with not just each other but with most of the life on this planet with advanced nervous systems and even some without. We need to eat. We need a certain amount of stability, usually in the form of territory that is ours, but also in relationships. We defend this turf and so does just about everything else. We get internal rewards for behavior which is likely to propagate our genes, and so does just about everything else — or it wouldn't be there. We investigate the territory around us, looking for more food, secure places, and ways to better our condition. Most other higher forms of life do this too. Individual survival is enhanced when a number of individuals cooperate in a common task and if the others in the group are healthy enough to do their share — something that goes both toward a form of altruism and toward its opposite. Survival has a logic that is independent of human feeling or philosophy.

This is not to claim that aliens who share none of these things are impossible, just that they are likely to be unusual.

Aliens, especially aliens that build and fly starships, will have minds that have been selected by the need of working effectively with matter. This probably means that they, or at least the ones that do this, will have discovered that matter obeys regular laws — rules sure enough to trust your life to. They will have gone through the process of discovering that planets and stars are not supernatural objects. They will have made many of those counterintuitive discoveries that reason and rules lead to.

This does not rule out supernatural beliefs, of course. But it does constrain and segregate those beliefs to an area of life that does not interfere with building and flying spaceships, or they would not be building and flying spaceships.

It isn't unlikely, though not certain, they have been through a process of having to overcome or finesse a previously established world view in order to do this. The history of technological progress is the history of rebellion against old ways of doing things and thinking about things in order to make things work. But it is also a history of giving very little credence to nonsense which closely resembles world views that don't work.

I expect spacefaring cultures will carry with them histories of their own Galileos and Darwins and thus a certain amount of sympathy for those beset by the sort of persecution that goes with upsetting dogma.

And I suspect the need for security in our species will continue to generate people who feel lost in the face of the complex realities of the material world and are willing to abandon this cultural birthright for a group that promises a prosperous way of life and simple answers for the things that matter — as long as you don't question too closely.

The range of human belief and behavior is very broad, and I see no reason for us to be unique in this respect. We may have a different "center" based on our biological and cultural heritage. But some of us and some of them will have been down many of the same roads and our culture will overlap with theirs in many ways. And those in the overlap areas will likely get along better with their alien counterparts than with some of the diverse elements of their own culture.

In "Comet Gypsies" there are no biological aliens to provide a contrast — but it is about alienation, just as, while it never gets to Mars, it is also about the process of making Mars habitable.

A WORLD TO BUILD

"**T**HIS PLANET'S SURFACE," Eldest Daughter announced, "has spent most of its existence under a near vacuum."

Althor, in a hundred revolutions plus of existence, was no longer easily surprised, but this was a little more of a surprise than most. He slowed his walker to a pace that permitted conversation, but rather than reply with specific aural symbols, he allowed a breath filled with the low frequency tones of doubt and uncertainty to escape through his ear holes.

"Cosmic rays, Hive-Father," she answered, almost shrill in her certainty. "There was no atmosphere thick enough to block the primary rays for the two and a half billion revolutions."

"Eldest Daughter, extraordinary claims require extraordinary proof. Sapients evolved on this world — we can trace the fossil history. And we have evidence of protozoans in rocks almost as old as the planet itself!"

"But nothing on the surface for almost three billion revolutions."

"Are you implying the atmosphere is a construct? Done by the oldest race?"

Her tentacles waved in uncertainty. "That, or it was done for them. Come to think of it, the fossil record has seemed a bit unusual, jumping from protozoan things to sophisticated multicellular creatures in the blink of a geological eye."

Wordlessly, he signaled his walker onward. After several trips to the surface and a program of exercises in the high gravity extension of their ring city, the pull of this planet's surface had begun to bother him less. He would not claim to be comfortable, but there was something about being in the open on solid ground with a real horizon in the distance that felt liberating.

He thought. A *made* world? No, it had been there from the system's origin. But a *made* atmosphere? In a way it made sense. But...

"Eldest Daughter, there were floods, storms, and silt layers here billions of revolutions before the earliest evidence of the oldest ones."

"This is true, but the atmosphere may have been only temporary, in the geological sense. The planet has no magnetic field to speak of, so the exobase would have been exposed directly to the stellar wind. Any atmosphere would have been carried off in a few million revolutions, I think."

Althor, whose brain resided near his stomach, shared his species difficulty in distinguishing an overloaded brain from a mild case of indigestion. As usual, though, it only took him a few moments of concentrated thought to come up with the answer.

"Then that's the explanation!"

"What, Hive-Father?"

"Fast adaptive radiation! Each time this world developed an atmosphere, its life developed a little further — they would have had a higher mutation rate due to exposure to the cosmic radiation and this star's ultraviolet light. In the final cycle, the inhabitants developed intelligence, space travel, and the cybernetic machinery needed to keep the atmosphere from leaking away again."

This time, Eldest daughter stopped her walker.

"Got you there!" Althor felt better. For many revolutions now, Eldest Daughter had clearly been running things. If she kept on this way, she would go into sex change involuntarily and the two of them would not be able to stand being in sight of each other. But if he maintained some semblance of dominance...

"Hive-Father, do you see what is weathering out of the cliff over there?"

It took a while to recognize it, for it was definitely not what he was looking for. It jutted out from the sandstone, broken, yes, but very large, clearly curved, and clearly artificial. As his brain finally coiled its mental tendrils around it, he saw more structure below. It looked, he admitted, exactly like the structures his own people had built on their airless worlds, to keep the air in.

So, not only were his people not alone, they were not alone in shaping worlds to fit their fancy.

"What kind of folk," Eldest Daughter said in her most reverent tones, "put air on this world?"

COMET GYPSIES

"TIME TO PACK the kitchen, darling. We're done with lunch." Yeah, Celinda thought, the last meal was over and it was time to pull her things off the wall and help the habitat cyberservant put everything in mothballs.

"I'll be right there," she shouted from amidst boxes labeled 'Deimos Storage' and 'BRS *Jan Oort*' "I just want to get this stain off the coffee table."

She wanted everything to look fresh when they moved into the next habitat. A quick spray and a little elbow grease with a durowipe brought a sparkle back to its diamond coat, and made the initials carved in the stone face below stand out as clearly as if they'd been carved yesterday. But it was forty years and three comets ago, now. Funny, though, she could close her eyes and it seemed like yesterday.

Oh, Willie, she thought. If you could only have been there that last week....

♂ ♂ ♂

"Dad," she'd complained, waving at craters and hills around her, "won't there be *anything* left?"

She'd grown up here, played in their comet's crystal caves with Willie and Peetie, thrown rocks into eccentric orbits over pitted plains, grown her own garden in a large plastic sphere, and built a space colony for her dolls. Fifteen was getting a little old for doll houses, she realized, but when the vent tube that she had so carefully carved and lined with tiny trees and houses, had disappeared into the maw of the refinery feeding robot, she felt more than a twinge of nostalgia and regret.

"No, Celinda, they decided to change the trajectory a little so they can reuse the habitat. *Democritus* will use what's left of the comet as a tether sling reaction mass. Now, I know it's hard to say goodbye, but that's the way thing go. You've just got to look ahead."

"Yeah, I understand."

"Look, someday, twenty years from now, *Democritus* will intercept another comet, and another family will ride in on it with him. Maybe even yours!"

"I guess that's better than nothing." 'Tether sling reaction' told the story, the remains of the comet would go nearer the sun so the habitat would pass further away. Her playground would be evaporated, her crystal caves collapsed, her towers melted into puddles. She'd wanted to believe that a few craters, or maybe the rock house, would survive so that if she ever passed by it again she could put it on a viewscreen, point out a few things and say "Hey, that's where I grew up." Not fair. The habitat would survive, but her room would be someone else's room. *Democritus* would be someone else's cyberservant. Best forget, if she could.

"Do I really *have* to go to Earth?" she asked again.

Her father was silent, and raised his hand to scratch his head the way he did when he was trying to say something she didn't want to hear in a way that wouldn't sound too mean. He stopped the gesture before he hit his vacuum helmet, and she giggled. He let the hand relax to a neutral position.

"Yes. Your mother and I kind of hoped that you'd *want* to go, to see where we came from, to meet your aunt and your cousins, and all of that. I know this doesn't interest you very much just yet, but someday you'll remember and be very glad you came."

"But, that's how I feel about our comet. So does Peetie. So where will *our* home be?"

Her dad waved at the stars cascading across Orion and Canis Major down to the Southern Cross. "Out here. You can feel at home wherever you can see the stars."

"That's too, too *wide*. I can't touch the stars."

"No, not yet, I guess. Look, dear. Other things will come into your life and it won't matter so much. You just have to have patience and find them. And as for Peetie," Dad chuckled, "he wants to ride horses, not comets."

"Come on, Dad, that was three years ago. He wants to go out and explore Eris now."

Dad laughed. "I don't think he's going to make that expedition, but maybe he'll get a chance at Alpha Centauri, if he does his studies. Now, young lady, we've got to get ready for the rendezvous team. They're going to be here in um... thank you, *Democritus*... four hours. The beam projector is going to fire in about an hour, if you want to watch?"

Democritus had told her that the transition team included two unattached young men. Of course she wanted to watch, and be there when they arrived.

"Maybe," she said, with feigned indifference. "Of course, I've got some studying to do."

"Well, you can check your own suit now. I'm going over to the projector site and look over *Democritus'* shoulder a bit. See you later, Ceecie."

She winced when he called her that. "Celinda, Dad!"

"Sorry, Celinda, I forgot." He gave her a vacuum-gloved squeeze on her shoulder. "Maybe I was getting a bit nostalgic myself. Well, later." He nodded, released his boot claws, and gave a jump away from the billion-ton remnant of their comet toward the trillion ton frozen water sphere where the beam projector was mounted. Dad always checked up on what *Democritus* was doing; he said human beings could usually think of more things that could go wrong.

The water iceball was a brilliant crescent from Celinda's vantage point, and its shadows hid the other spheres strung out behind it. She remembered the day, on her tenth birthday, when the big, smooth, impersonal iceball became bigger than her shrinking comet. Everyone celebrated, but she had been a bit sad because it meant that her home and playground was shrinking. She christened the iceball "Vampira" because it was sucking the life out of her comet, and Willie had drawn a face on a yellow apple, stuck two toothpicks where the teeth would be, and given it to her.

"Vampira" would, of course, get its comeuppance when it shattered into shards, got vaporized by the Martian atmosphere, and turned into so much rain. She smiled wickedly at the thought of it melting down like the Wicked Witch of the West.

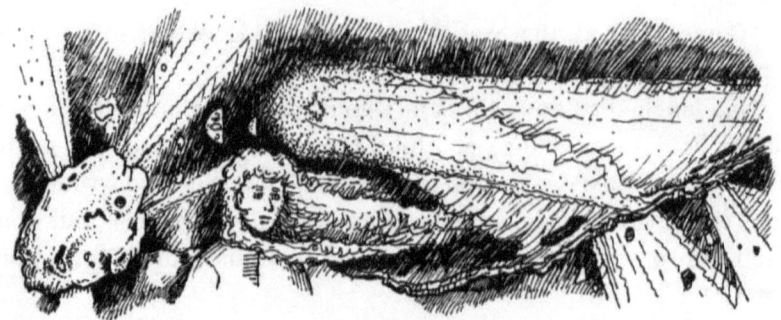

She reached down, picked up a piece of comet dust, and watched it sit there until she could tell for sure that it was slowly drifting back to the ground. The first time she'd done that, before Peetie was born, when it had just been Mom, Dad, and her, the piece of comet actually fell back to the ground, though slowly. But there was hardly any 'ground' left. Hardly any falling happened now.

Mom would be getting dinner ready for company, and probably wanted her to help with the vegetables. She rocked on her toes to release herself and jumped for the habitat elevator. She grabbed the axis bar in a fluid motion, hung on with one finger as it brought her up to the habitat's leisurely rotational speed, then pushed herself into the elevator cage. "Down, *Democritus*."

♂ ♂ ♂

Celinda came up with Mom to watch the docking, after all. The magnetic sailship, still many kilometers distant, looked like a tiny, exquisite double engagement ring to her; one with stones on either side. It was glowing in the middle where its lasers ionized the atoms *Democritus* was throwing at it — and bouncing them back for thrust.

"*Democritus* says there are a couple of single guys on that ship," Celinda hinted, hoping Mom knew more.

"It's a family crew, dear, like we are. Its captain is Tara Van Doren — I think she's from Peary Crater on Luna. She has two sons, a daughter, a son-in-law, and a grandchild along with her."

"Mom..."

"The *unattached* sons are fifteen and twenty-three. Now remember what..."

"I'm not going to be a pest. I just want to *talk* with someone."

"Uh-huh. Dear, I just want you to know that if it gets to be more than that, I'm your friend, not your judge. We have to keep communications open. I was younger than you are when I..."

"It's okay, Mom. I'm not on that vector. Besides, they're only going to be here for a week and then I'll never see them again. So it would be pretty dumb to get involved, huh?" Before Mom could agree, she changed the subject. "Uh, what happened to Ms. Van Doren's husband?"

"I don't know, and don't *you* ask. If she or her children want to say anything, they will do that on their own. Otherwise it's none of your business."

"Okay, Roger. I read you."

Her mother laughed and squeezed her hand. Parents doing a lot of squeezing today, she thought.

The arrival of the magnetic sailship took all afternoon. They watched from the shadow of the comet, where their eyes could adapt to the dark. With pupils wide open, they could see the delicate plume of the reflected ions mimic the tail of an untamed comet, stretching many kilometers across the stars. Then the two "stones" on opposite sides of the ring glowed brilliantly.

"Why are they so bright?" Peetie asked her.

"There's a lot of energy tied up in the magnetic field," she said. "It has to go somewhere when they turn it off — so they turn it into light."

"Why do they have to turn the magnetic field off?"

"To keep the solar wind from blowing them away."

"Why doesn't it blow us away?"

"Because we don't have a big magnetic field. Just the habitat shielding."

"What happens after they get here?"

"They send the iceballs to Mars and a couple of other places, help us pack up and take us away. Everything's going to change."

"What about here?"

Celinda groaned. "Peetie, there won't be any here, *here* anymore." Why didn't Mom or Dad tell him first, Celinda wondered. Her parents were letting her do all the explaining and she was just as unhappy about leaving as Peetie. "Comets aren't forever, Peetie. Look! See the thrusters firing?"

"I don't... Oh. Yeah. They're like little stars."

"Yeah." She gave him a little squeeze. Moving with a sort of stately grace, squirting jets of fire here and there, the visitor settled into the lazy orbit around the "Vampira" iceball train their habitat shared with the remnant of the comet. A skycycle detached itself from the spacecraft and headed for the landing dock. Celinda's suit warned her that its power level was down to seventy-five percent — she'd been out here, watching the show, for almost three hours and would need to put it on the charger when she got back.

"Can we play in the ice-flower cave?" Peetie asked.

"It's gone, Peetie. Vampira ate it yesterday morning."

"Why?"

"So, just like everything else, they can sort out all the molecules and add them to the iceballs that are going to Mars."

"I know that. Why can't they make an exception for special cases."

"It's all going to melt anyway. They're going to change the orbit after we're gone."

"How about the cave where Willie..."

"That's gone too."

"Oh. Did they have to..."

"Yes."

"What about the rock house. They didn't eat the rock house, did they?"

"No it's still there."

The fort was at the comet's north pole, the last place to be savaged by Vampira's helpers. But the robots were almost there, and had a few more days to do their vile work. She and Willie had started it, piling boulders up and tacking them in place with vacuum tape and frozen mud until they'd had a rough-hewn fairy castle with a watchtower soaring a hundred meters up toward the stars. Dad called it the tower of baffle because, he said, whatever kept it up baffled him.

"Celinda," her Mom called, "we need to go back now and get ready for our visitors. Take care of Peter and don't be late, please. I want you looking really nice."

"Sure, Mom."

"Can we go see the rock house before the robots eat it?" Peetie begged.

"Okay, but be careful. There's so little gravity left that it might fly apart if you push it."

That turned out to be a bit of an exaggeration. While there was only a kilometer of comet left, most of it was dense silica and siderophilic slag. *Democritus* said they had one ten-thousandth of a gee. So, she thought, a ten ton boulder still weighed a newton, and the main tower — with over two thousand taped and freeze mortared boulders now — still weighed more than either of them could lift. They grabbed a handyline and pulled themselves to the playground. Celinda gave a bottom boulder of the rock house a few experimental pushes, and it felt reasonably solid. Then she stared at the boulder she'd pushed a long while.

"What are you looking at?" Peetie asked.

"This was the first rock," Celinda told him. "Dad lasered its face flat. I think we called it the cornerstone, even though the tower's a circle with no corner."

"That's silly."

"Yeah. Anyway, we cut our initials in it. See?" She brushed off the dust that clung to everything left unattended for a while and shined a light on the smooth face. It was, she realized, the first time she'd cleaned it off since Willie died. "W.I. for Willie. C.I for me. L.I. for dad. 2111 was the year."

"I never saw that! Eleven years ago. That's as old as I am! So where's Mom's initials?"

"She wasn't here then, she was back in the habitat."

"Where's my initials?"

"You're *why* she wasn't here, Peetie," Celinda laughed. "She had to feed the baby."

♂ ♂ ♂

They were late, of course. By the time Peetie had gotten his fill of extending the west ramparts, and got to the elevator just as the visitors arrived.

"Hi," she said. "This is Peter and I'm Celinda." She held out a glove to one of two people whose helmet read 'A. Van Doren.'

"Avram Van Doren, a man's voice replied. My brother's using my spare helmet — Mike?"

"Zoned, Celinda," the other person labeled 'A. Van Doren' said with a phony sneer in his voice. "and here's the dino that runs the show. Mom? Some comet meat is here to greet." The final member of the transition team had stayed to double check the skycycle tie-down, and was just joining them.

"Oh, we have a welcoming committee! I'm Tara... and you're Celinda... and you're Peetie, right?" The woman shook hands with each of them, Peetie last.

"Peter, really," he said. "They just call me that because I'm little."

Was there a note of irritation in Peetie's voice? Celinda looked at her brother, and noted that the top of his helmet was up to her chin. The last time she'd noticed, he'd come up to about where her breasts were — before she had them. More changes.

"My apologies, young man." Tara Van Doren murmured with good humor. "Well, we shouldn't keep your family waiting, should we? Would you do the honors, Celinda?"

"Oh, sure." She'd forgotten to tell *Democritus* to start the elevator down, and he'd wait for orders from a family member if one was present. It felt funny to give the orders with adults around, but she said 'Down, *Democritus*' just like she would have done if it had only been Peetie and her. Mike, the fifteen-year-old, asked a lot of questions on the way down. In a way, he reminded her of Willie, kind of roly-poly without being really fat, full of energy and maybe a little impatient about things in general. The memory gave her a little chill. And the way he looked at her when she peeled off her shipsuit in the airlock — it was like he'd never seen a girl in a sprayshirt and shorties before.

Mom frowned at her when they emerged and Celinda felt instantly guilty; she should have been back earlier and dressed up for the company. Mom herself was wearing a jet black jumpsuit with white stripes on the outer seams with a sparkling diamond pin that Celinda had never seen before. She'd seen Mom and Dad dress up for dinner once in a while, for the fun of it, but *this* was an eye-opener. What was going on? Celinda wondered, and looked to see how their guests were dressed.

Mike and Avram were wearing standard gray shipsuits and carrying overnight bags, but when Captain Tara Van Doren got out of her vacuum overclothes, Celinda understood why all the dress-up. This woman, a grandmother according to Dad, and who talked in what Celinda thought was a kind of grandmotherly way, looked like a classic model or a video star. Celinda stared wide-eyed at Captain Van Doren's strong facial bones, big eyes, smooth skin, and perfect figure. Her midnight blue shipsuit had a dramatic wide white diagonal stripe and her straight frosty-blond hair hung just above her shoulders with a hint of a wave.

Captain Van Doren returned Celinda's stare with a smile, and looked even younger, except for her eyes — which looked mature in a way that Celinda couldn't define. The effect was regal. No wonder Mom had wanted Celinda to get dressed — not that anything Celinda had would make her look like that!

Celinda grinned and shrugged her shoulders. So Mike and Avram probably had unreasonable expectations; it wasn't like she was desperate or anything. And, except for Mom, everyone seemed to ignore the fact that Celinda looked like she'd just finished helping *Democritus* clean out a hydroponics tank. So she resolved to carry on as if nothing was amiss.

Avram flashed her a quick friendly smile, but hardly said anything. He was a bit shorter than his brother, but looked taller because he had a lankier build, and he seemed much more reserved. When she shook his hand, it seemed different, somehow, and the surprise must have shown on her face.

"It's artificial." He smiled at her, almost shyly. "I lost the real one a while back."

"I'm sorry, I didn't mean to, you know..."

"Space." He invoked the word that explained everything, and flashed that boyish grin at her again. "Doesn't bother me."

"The baby won't be any problem," she overheard Mom say to Captain Van Doren. A baby! Her memories of Peetie as a baby were eleven years old, and she hardly remembered Willie that way at all.

"You have a baby?" she asked Avram, making no attempt to conceal her excitement.

"My sister, Tonya, has a baby. It's sleeping now. Tonya and Ed are helping *Dr. Zarkhov* finish our propulsion shut-down. They'll all be down for dinner."

The baby was all Celinda could think of while she gave the Van Doren brothers a tour of their habitat, which was fortunate because Mike's groundheaded questions were a little irritating.

"Why," he complained as they took the elevator down to the living quarters, "do you have your house so far from the spin center? We live fifty meters from our spin center and it's just fine that way. Everything's so heavy here, it's like being on Mars!"

"Dad likes it that way — he says we weren't built to spin as fast as a lot of people do, and if we don't spin so much, we don't need to take as many pills. But after we get packed and you guys send the iceballs on their way, we're going to spin faster — to get ready for Earth."

That got Mike's attention. "You're going to Earth? Why? When?"

"For our education, Dad says. And he and Mom want to visit where they grew up." For a moment, Celinda felt sense of jealousy and overwhelming loss. She'd never be able to go home.

"What's wrong?" Avram asked, concerned in his eyes and the set of his lips. Full lips, those.

Celinda realized she had a tear on her face.

"I don't know. I guess it's about everything changing and ending. I'm sorry. Look, we're at the family level now." The interior elevator descended into their circular livingroom, which *Democritus* had neat and tidy. The costume she'd been sewing was nowhere in sight — probably dumped on her bed to clear the room. She stepped off the elevator stage and invited the others to follow.

"This is it?" Mike asked. "You lived in this can for fifteen years?

"Nothing but vacuum below the floor." An imp got into her; she stomped her foot hard on the floor and it gave satisfying a hollow ring. Mike suddenly got a worried look on his face, and his brother got a twinkle in his eye. "Except," Celinda continued, "about a meter of aluminum honeycomb, conduits, and a meteor shield covered with magnetic coils and laser rock-blasters."

They all laughed. She remembered how scared *she'd* been when Willie had body-slammed her in that very spot, right in front of her horrified Dad, after threatening to throw her through the floor for cleaning up the concert poster collection he'd left out. She'd bounced back intact, and the only hurt was her memory of the awful things she'd said to Willie. If she could only have those words back.

"Uh, would you guys like to catch a newscast or listen to something while I get ready for dinner."

"Can I peep your zone?" piped Mike, leering.

Was he serious? She'd had fantasies about modeling, art, and acting, and knew that sometimes meant using one's bare body, and the idea of guys looking at her hadn't bothered her that much, in principle, until now.

But the way Mike said that made her feel more like a clathrate specimen than a beautiful person. Creepy. Before she could think of anything to say, his brother coughed loudly and gave him a mean look. If looks could kill ...

"Just joking," Mike quickly added, with a pout and little frightened laugh. Oh. Battered brother syndrome, she judged, and felt instantly sorry for him, despite his feigned crudity.

She shrugged her shoulders. "If you want entertainment, we're less than half an AU above Ceres, and we've been getting their regional broadcasts for the last month. I caught the Ceres Philharmonic doing Zhou's tenth symphony last night, it's in our current file."

"Yuck," Mike said. "*Pre*-Mesozoic! How about the Nukes? You got Nukes? I wanna fireball!"

The Cretin! Celinda thought. She knew what he meant, but pretended to deliberately misunderstand. "We have a dozen half megaton orbit-adjust charges left. For the iceballs."

"I'd like to help you place put one in his ear," Avram offered. "Though it might not be loud enough for his taste."

You shouldn't talk to your brother like that, Celinda thought... even when it's justified.

"Aw, recycle a pill, bro," Mike whined.

"Mike, there's some of Willie's stuff on the cribbage board," Celinda offered quickly, gesturing to the rack of music sticks in their bookcase. "It's all over two years old, but maybe there's something you like. The blue earphones were his, they're calibrated for that stuff, so blow your brains out if you like." She smiled to make sure he took that the right way. He gave her a little twisted grin back. She turned to his brother.

"Avram, We've got holizations of space drama going back two hundred fifty years. We have all of Johansen's zero-gee ballet back to early twenty-first century. Opera, too if you're interested. The green earphones are mine, so feel free to use them. *Democritus* can play-back anything you guys want, simultaneously or whatever. So just ask."

Then she looked Mike in the eye and called his bluff. "As far as watching me change clothes, I think that's kind of strange. Celinda Ivanov isn't worth it. Especially when you can watch a holo of Dame Gweneth Jones as *Salome*, or Leslie Inowei in *The Moonrider's Mistress*. But I'm not shy." She tossed her head to indicate her indifference. "Watch if you like."

The expression on Avram's face was disturbed but unreadable.

Celinda sighed.

"Actually, we need to change, too," Avram said. Where's your head?"

"Huh? Oh. Uh, use Willie's room. It's the door just to the right of the door with all the garish stuff. *That's* Peetie's room." Peetie made a face. "Make yourselves at home," she added.

Avram turned as if to ask her something, and for a moment she was afraid, or maybe hoped, the question might be 'I see the room but, where's Willie?' Then she could explain and get it off her chest. But they didn't ask, any more than she would ask, 'where's Mr. Van Doren?'

She walked into her room and found herself saying "leave the door open," to *Democritus*, feeling that she was going to be nice to brothers, regardless of whose brothers they were, regardless of how silly their wants were. Considering how she ran around most of the time, It was no big deal.

Then she forgot all about it. There, spread out on her bed, was her classic 'Star Trek' uniform, finished to perfection. She'd look just like Uhura, well, allowing for a slight difference in age. The uniform was patterned after the one Celinda's heroine, Nichelle Nichols, wore as an admiral in her last film in 2021, over a century ago. Celinda loved costumes; she'd been Annie Oakley, Hatshepsut, Athena, Commander Erin Wu, Donna Elvira, Jeanne D'Arc, and last year she and Mom had designed matching Maria Theresa gowns with huge wigs.

"*Democritus*, who got you to do that? It's beautiful. Wow!"

"Your mother did that by hand, not me. She wanted it to be a surprise for you, before the Van Doren's came."

Celinda shut her eyes. Why had she stayed outside so long when she'd promised to be back? Peetie was why. "Tell Mom I love her, and I'm sorry I stayed out with Peetie so long."

She almost flew into the tiny shower between her room and her parents, soaped herself, washed off the sprayshirt with a chemical sponge, peeled off the shorties, wrung them out, and clipped them in front of the recovery grid to dry out. This was all done in about a minute, so she had about a minute to luxuriate in the needle spray before the dry cycle kicked in. The warm hurricane had her dry in twenty sensual seconds.

She gave her tangled, curly, shoulder-length hair a few perfunctory brushes and bounded for the costume on the bed. It was sheer heaven to put on, full of fresh feels and fresh smells. It molded itself around her with only a little tug here and there. She admired herself in her wall screen, then turned for the door.

And was surprised by a round of applause. There were Mike — leering, Peetie — wide eyed, and Avram — looking somewhat embarrassed, but looking, nevertheless.

She shook her head, looked at the ceiling, and said "Beam me *up*, Scotty."

Dinner was cultured chicken breast marinated in wine they made from their own grapes, topped with a yeast-based white sauce and served with slices of their own zucchini and tomatoes. Celinda helped *Democritus'* motiles take the stuff up to the dining area they'd set up in the garden.

"Your farm is miraculous, Larry," Avram said. It was a bit unnerving to Celinda to here Avram call Dad by his first name. He was about midway between Dad and her in age, but she'd kind of been classifying Avram on her side of the line. That was silly, of course — Captain Van Doren didn't run the operation herself — Mike and the granddaughter were the only excess mass.

"Celinda has the green thumb," Dad said, and ostentatiously reached over, plucked a ripe tomato from the vine, and started to slice it. She gave him smile.

"Mom should really get some credit, too," she added with feigned modesty. She was *proud* of that garden.

"Mmmm." Avram said, over a tomato slice.

"She had it going before I took over. Really, I just help *Democritus*. He gets the light, the nutrients, and all the cycles right. I just look at the individual plants and tell him if one needs a little more, here or there."

Avram nodded. "People are still better than artificial intelligence in making subjective visual judgments. They're also better at creating solutions to non-standard problems, when they know the subject fairly well."

"I'd say Celinda is pretty good at both," Avram's sister, Tonya, added. Celinda thought that, in a sort of natural way, she was as pretty as Captain Van Doren.

"Yeah," Mike chimed in. "well, she's got scales." Celinda couldn't figure out whether that was a complement or a slam, coming from Mike. "Do you make any beer?" he wanted to know.

"We don't have a lot of grain, because it takes up a lot of space — we use cultures for most of our meat and starch. The farm is mainly for veggies. But we'll have real escargot tomorrow."

"Yuck," Mike said.

Captain Van Doren rolled her eyes and smiled apologetically. Avram looked troubled.

"Well," Dad entered the conversation with that I've-got-a-surprise look in his eye. "It looks like we're going to go ahead and launch the glassball — to!"

"Huh?" Celinda, Mom, and Peetie said almost together. The others grinned. Peetie got kind of frown on his face that he gets when he doesn't understand why everyone else is confused.

Celinda broke the silence. "Okay, Dad. I'll bite. Pluto isn't Mars. It's way back out where we came from. Why Pluto? Mars is a lot closer."

Dad raised his eyebrows like he did when he wanted someone else to answer; someone like her. She was supposed to figure this out... but her mind was absolutely blank.

"Yes," Avram said, coming to her rescue. "It's closer in space, but not closer in energy, which is what really counts. It's a lot easier to get something to Pluto with our velocity vector than it is to match velocity with Mars. It's all right for the iceballs to burn in and evaporate, but that's dangerous with the hard stuff. Besides, Mars already has enough sand. On Pluto, they need all that silicon, aluminum, and trace elements for building material for the scientific base they're building, and you've already sorted and refined a billion tons of it. It ought to get there in about thirty years, just in time for their next addition."

"But the rest of it *is* going to Mars, isn't it?" Peetie asked, with a protest in his voice. It's hard, Celinda reflected, to learn something one hour only to have to unlearn it the next.

"Of course, the ice, carbon dioxide, the methane, and the nitrogen are all going to Mars," Captain Van Doren replied. "We have to wait a day or so for the right time to kick those out."

"I understand," Celinda said.

"I don't," Mike objected. "I don't know why we're doing any of this when we could be back on Earth or Mars living like normal people. This whole thing sucks, even if Celinda has a crude bod — and *she's* a dinosaur. Eighty per of the human race is laid back in their zones cooling it while the bots feed'em, but *we* have to run around out in nowhere doing nothing but work, work, work. It sucks!"

Celinda felt so embarrassed, she wanted to drop right through four floors to her room.

Captain Van Doren smiled again, tightly, and laughed gently, though the laugh had an edge. "If you could phrase that differently, dear, these people might need a translation. In fact I might need one too."

"What you need, old lady, is a..."

"Mike!" Avram interrupted, with a sharp threat in his voice, drowning out whatever word Mike used.

"...and so do you, *Ceecie*. You wanna *do*, I can tell, and if you'd blast Nuke instead of living in the age of reptiles, you'd get what you want!"

Celinda shot a look at Peetie, who tried to hide. Telling childhood nicknames was out of bounds, and he knew it. Then she looked Mike straight in the eye to show that she wasn't afraid, intimidated by him, or really that much bothered by his clumsily offensive effort to deny his biological attraction to her, and the vulnerability it implied. She felt a little sorry for him.

"Young man," Dad rumbled, as softly and seriously as she had ever heard him, "you are a guest here, and while you are here you must respect *our* code of social behavior. Which is not that of the Nukes. Understand? *Democritus*, place a motile behind Mikhail Van Doren."

Celinda winced, but kept quiet. Mike seemed surprised, then turned around to see the motile, which had silently assumed its station.

"Dad wouldn't let you get away with that!" he complained.

Captain Van Doren suddenly looked not thirty, but about seventy. "I… hope nothing like that will be necessary. Mikhail, please try to be more polite."

"Or they'll chop me up and feed me to those bots? Fat chance! If my Dad were here…"

Celinda's caught *her* Dad whisper something under his breath and just like that, the motile's hands were suddenly on Mike's shoulders. The cockiness vanished from his face and he looked around for help, and, not finding any, settled back and said "Ouch. Okay, okay."

Dad said, "I think we need to talk privately, Tara. Later."

The woman looked miserable, and nodded.

Mike left the table without saying anything. The motile stayed.

Tonya's husband, who had remained silent all the way through incident cleared his throat and mentioned some of the more interesting trades done on the glassball's Pluto trajectory. To Celinda's great relief, they spend the rest of the evening discussion the orbital maneuvers.

♂ ♂ ♂

After dinner, Celinda finally got to see the baby. Tonya invited her down to their study on the third deck, which had been converted to a nursery for the duration of the Van Doren's stay. There, Celinda was able to change little Theodor, and watch Tonya feed him. She did the latter very naturally, without any sense of embarrassment at Celinda's curiosity.

"It's so beautiful," Celinda gushed, and got a warm smile in return.

"Celinda," Tonya began, softly, "about my brother…"

"It's okay. I can take it. Willie was a kind of like that…"

"Willie, yes." The older woman frowned briefly, then looked at Celinda as if she were really interested. "Do you want to talk about it?"

"I guess you've kind of noticed that Willie isn't here anymore."

Tonya nodded again. Her baby fussed a bit, and she switched sides.

"He was a couple of years younger than I was. He was a lot of fun as a little kid — we wrestled, played hide and seek, word games, and everything. But as we got older, we didn't get along — he needed so much, well, stimulation. Loud music. Violent videos. War toys. He was always doing something to get attention, to challenge the rest of us — bizarre haircuts patterned after some Earth fad, dirty language, anything he could do that was hostile and attention getting. We were always arguing about spacesuit safety and self-discipline. He'd ignore me."

Tonya nodded sympathetically. "There are certain lifestyles that just don't fit on a family spaceship. You have to watch where your feelings are leading you, and think first. Even then..." a momentary frown passed Tonya's face. "But what happened to Willie?"

"We went out one day to explore what was left of the comet. That was about the only thing we could still do together. That and work on the rock house. We were in this cave, and I was giving him a big sister lecture about keeping his back unit clean. He got mad at me, said don't be such a reptile — that the stuff was built to take it. Then he took his unit off and rolled it around in the comet dust just to show me."

A tear trickled down Celinda's face now. Tonya reached for a clean diaper and handed it to her. "They're absorbent."

Celinda half giggled, and blotted her face. "Well, Willie got some grit in the connector, and it wouldn't reconnect. I tried to get him to go back to the habitat — you can last five or six minutes on the air in your helmet if you're careful." She took a deep breath, remembering, and thinking about how nice it was to be able to breathe.

Tonya nodded.

Celinda continued. "He wouldn't go. He kept trying to shake the dust out of his connector. I called *Democritus* for help. Then he got mad and tried to jam the connector on — and broke it. I got the buddy hose out of the bottom of my pack, so we could share my air until help arrived. But he'd already damaged the connector on his suit trying to jam the dirty connector in."

"Oh, dear," Tonya offered, sympathetically. Theodor was getting restless again, and Tonya bounced him a bit.

Celinda's mind took time out with the distraction. Babies, she remembered reading, bounced at different rhythms in different gravities. Someone had tried to do a study on whether there was an optimum baby bouncing frequency, and what gravity that corresponded to.

"Your brother suffocated? Right in front of you, like that?"

The question brought her back. Celinda shook her head and couldn't say anything for a few seconds. Then she took a deep breath and continued. "*Democritus* could have saved him if he'd just kept still. I tried to wiggle the hose onto the connector, but he said I wasn't trying hard enough, batted my hand away, and tried to force it on. Then he said the buddy hose didn't work right. For all I knew at the time, he was right, so I suggested he try his own buddy hose.

"Then it turned out that he'd cannibalized his own buddy hose for a fluid analog speaker, and lied to *Democritus* on the check out. So he spun me around and yanked my main hose out of my pack."

Tonya's eyes went wide, but Celinda shrugged. "He was getting short of air now, and wasn't thinking right. I don't blame him. It might have even worked — we could have shared air, buddy style, if he hadn't broken his suit connector."

Celinda stared at the floor, unable to watch Tonya's expression. "When it didn't work, he screamed. I tried to hold him and get him to calm down and be quiet, but he pushed me away. Then... then he got this wild look in his eye and picked up a rock. I backed further away. *Democritus* said he'd have an emergency air ball there in a minute, and that Mom and Dad were coming. If I could only have kept him quiet... But Willie yelled 'To hell with the universe, I'm going to destroy the universe and make it go away'."

"Oh, God. That's a Nukes lyric. Mike plays it all the time."

"I didn't know that — we wouldn't let Willie play his stuff on the speakers." Celinda took a breath. "He just took that rock, got this awful grin on his face, and smashed his own faceplate with it. I screamed until I ran out of oxygen and passed out myself. *Democritus* and Dad saved me, somehow. Sometimes I wish..."

Tonya held Celinda's hand tightly, and looked down on her baby, her face troubled.

Celinda was beyond sobbing now, and delivered the rest woodenly. "I was supposed to be taking care of Willie. I couldn't handle it. I killed my little brother by being... incompetent."

"No, no Celinda," Tonya got her attention, "it wasn't your fault. Please, look up."

She did, and Tonya's face was full of concern. Celinda looked at little Theodor. Maybe...

"Tonya, would you let an incompetent person hold your baby? Just for a bit?"

"I'll let Celinda Ivanov hold him, and I don't think she's a bit incompetent," Tonya laughed. "He's a bit messy, though. Drooly."

Celinda grinned, shrugged out of her costume tunic, and held little Theodor to her breast, skin on skin, letting him do what babies do, regardless of how little he got out of it. He seemed happy and skin was easy to clean. She fantasized that he was hers. She felt released and momentarily, very happy.

Celinda and Tonya took turns cuddling Theodor as they talked about Earth, boys, music, stars and babies. It was fairly late in their habitat's artificial evening when Tonya's husband knocked on the door, and Celinda bid the young family an embarrassed good night.

The habitat's interior lights were low when she left, and it looked like she was the last one up. She took the pole down from the third level to the fifth, much faster than the elevator. It dropped her right in front of the spare room, where Captain Van Doren was staying. There were voices inside — her father and the Captain. Probably working out some last minute details on iceball propulsion.

She was up early in the morning, sprayed-on an exercise outfit, shivering as the smart fibers at the edges crawled around to make their hems, and got to the gym before anyone else. *Democritus* fed her the day's lessons on a wall screen while she ran like Alice on the endless jogging rug. She was viewing a news dump about the first Martian crops when she became aware of someone else in the room. She turned and saw Avram.

"Hi," she said.

"Good morning." He gave her a quick smile and started slipping into a magnetic stress suit.

"Are you going to Earth too?" she asked.

"Not planning on it in the near future," he grunted as he stepped onto the solenoid stage and began his Tai Chi. "All the more reason to keep in shape. What's the limit on this set-up?"

"One point three, I think. It's supposed to take you up to two gravities, but Dad added a software stop because the field was interfering with some of his instruments. Uh, there are a couple loose magnets on that suit — on the elbow. I'm supposed to sew them on but I keep forgetting."

She remembered how Willie had torn the smart magnets off the suit in an angry reaction to banging his elbow one day. He'd been sure they'd pulled his arm into the wall, and no one had been able to convince him that the magnets couldn't pull him into a fiberglass wall, even if their orientation control was off, which it hadn't been. He'd yelled and cried and called them all liars. No need to tell Avram all that — he didn't seem to realize how precious little brothers were.

"Uh, won't your motiles…"

"I'm supposed to learn how to do this kind of stuff myself, so I won't feel so dependent on the cyberservants."

"Something wrong? Tonya mentioned you were upset about leaving."

She stopped jogging, coasted to the end of the rug, and turned toward him. "Yeah. Packing, leaving, going. Ghosts." They seemed to float in front of her eyes when she blinked, in front of all the conditioning equipment. One of them was a big five-year-old girl rocking her one-year-old brother in her arms. Hours and hours of rolling balls across the rug. That infection they both got that it took them two weeks to cure.

"Ghosts?!"

She shook her head. "Memories."

Then she started talking to Avram about her life on the comet, about how nice things had been just a few years ago with her, Willie, Mom, Dad and the baby. She told him how they'd played in the comet caves, or sat in a crater and watched the castle of tubes and cylinders where *Democritus* and his motiles refined the comet stuff into iceballs for Mars.

"Vampira ate that crater two, no, four years ago. But we have holos. Everything was so perfect then. But Willie started… changing. Or maybe not changing is more like it. You know, it was like he never could slow down and think about things, or make himself do the things you should do even if you don't feel like doing them. I mean, he was still my brother, and he could be a lot of fun in a spontaneous, outrageous, madcap sort of way. But that kind of thing gets scary on a comet."

"Or a spaceship," Avram agreed, "I know. Mike is a bit like that. Mom thinks it's because of what happened to Dad, but, I'm not sure. Maybe it's just him."

Avram appeared to lose interest in his exercises, turned down the magnetic field, and sat on the on the side solenoid stage. He gestured to the open space next to him.

Celinda sat down next to him, put her elbows on her knees and her chin in her hand. She knew she wasn't supposed to ask the question, but she judged that Avram wouldn't mind, and besides he knew all her private stuff now, so it was only fair.

"Do you want to talk about your father?" she asked, trying to sound as adult and sophisticated as Tonya had last night.

He looked at her and smiled. "You're curious about this?" he asked, and removed his left hand with his right, handing it to her, revealing a stump cap with a tiny red light in the middle.

"Oh!" She examined the prosthetic, curiosity getting the better of any social worries. "Uh. Sure. I mean that's kind of neat, gives a whole new meaning to the words 'optic nerve,' doesn't it? It doesn't hurt or anything, does it?"

Avram laughed softly. "No. Only when I think about how it happened."

She put two and two together. "You lost your hand when your father died?"

Avram nodded. "Yeah. We'd just finished transshipping an iceball to a lunar methane tanker. Mom had a social engagement lined up at Ceres for as soon as we reached orbit. She had just lost ten kilos and had some clothes that she thought would fit her again in a storage module on the other side of the ring." He shook his head. "If she could get them before we picked up the deceleration beam, she'd save an hour or so after we reached orbit. We were going through the belt with a relative velocity of forty kilometers per second. We could have sent a motile, but Dad felt cooped up and wanted to get out. I went along. We disabled the guard lasers for the trip so we wouldn't accidentally put a hand in front of one just as a piece of rock went by." He gave her a bitter smile. "Well, a piece of rock went by. We'd just gotten the container and closed the compartment. I felt a sharp tug on my wrist, like a cramp, then nothing. I actually reached for the container, didn't feel it then looked down at the stump, not believing it because I felt like I could still move my fingers. But it was gone. The stump was foaming blood in the vacuum, I got scared and couldn't remember what to do. I called to Dad."

Celinda put her hand on his real hand.

"Dad wasn't there," he finished. "*Dr. Zarkhov* found two pieces on radar, outbound at five klips."

Celinda nodded. "Space." she said. "How did you get back?"

"I pressed the stump into my stomach and ran along the inside of the ring. I lost consciousness before I cycled through the lock, but the motiles got me. It was a bit of a mess.

"Do you want to know something funny?"

It didn't sound very funny to Celinda, but an inner voice told her to listen instead of comment, so she just nodded.

"I was still holding onto the container with Mom's dress. They said I wouldn't let it go."

Celinda was quiet for a while, then asked "How long ago?"

"Two years. Mike's blamed Mom ever since, and she feels so guilty she lets him do anything he wants. I'm the one that has to say 'no,' and he hates *me* for that."

Celinda nodded. She knew that kind of hate. "Deep down, they know you mean the best for them. And they feel as bad about not fitting in as you do."

"They?"

"The ones that don't belong out here." Her voice was calm and adult, but her eyes were glistening. "The ones that should never have been out here in the first place, because of what's inside them. The Willies and the Mikes." There, she'd said it. She loved Willie — but he didn't belong.

"And Peetie?"

Celinda just shook her head. "Too early to tell. I can still cuddle him and... Say, would you let me put your hand back on?"

He nodded and showed her how. She wanted to do something intimate, and, well, that seemed to work for her. Besides, it was a clever piece of engineering.

Democritus interrupted them.

"Avram, Celinda. We have an emergency. Mikhail and Peter are in trouble outside. People are meeting at the top level, by the air lock."

Celinda jumped up and started out the gym door, then, remembering that Avram was unfamiliar with their habitat, turned, said "this way" leading him to the right; away from the elevator and toward the pole. They were both in good shape and could use their arms to haul themselves up much faster than the elevator could have.

When they reached the top level, they found both families clustered around the airlock. Tonya's husband, who had said so little at dinner the night before that Celinda couldn't remember his name was putting on vacuum overclothes. "Avram," he called out as soon as the younger man popped up the pole hatch, "suit up. The auxiliary skycycle's already chasing them, we're going to follow."

"What happened?" Celinda said, "Where's Peetie?"

Her mother rushed over to her and started to smother her. Celinda grabbed her hands.

"Mom, what happened?"

"The Van Doren's skycycle ran away, dear. Mike was bored and he was taking it back to their ship to listen to his music where nobody would bother him about the noise. Peetie was with Mike."

"I want to go after him, Mom." Celinda ran for her shipsuit and helmet. "Please?"

"Celinda!" her Father's voice was sharp. He was clearly going to object.

"Larry," Avram interrupted, "she's lighter. That'll give the cycle more delta vee."

Tonya looked Celinda's father in the eye and pleaded her case silently. Dad tightened his lips, and gave a nod. "Very well. If it's all right with Greg."

That was Tonya's husband's name, Celinda remembered now. She felt a momentary hesitation. She needed to be there for Peetie, to try to make up for losing Willie. But she hadn't thought far enough ahead to realize that would mean bumping Tonya's husband from the rescue mission.

But he smiled gallantly. "Tonya told me, Celinda. And I hear that you're as good a cometeer as they come. *Dr. Zarkhov* will be looking out for you too, so it should be safe enough. As safe as anything out here."

Everyone was silent on that for a second, but Celinda kept getting dressed. The shipsuit fitted over her athletic sprays easily enough. *Democritus* had her overclothes ready, and she was running a goo-smeared finger around the inside of her neck seal by the time Mom broke the silence.

"I'll talk to you later, Larry," she said sharply, and headed for the elevator.

Dad looked pained. Captain Van Doren came over and placed her hand on his arm. They looked at each other briefly, then Dad looked Celinda in the eyes.

"Keep your head, young lady. Maximum effort until everyone's safe. Understand."

"Yeah, Dad. I'm good to go." They gave each other a thumbs up.

Democritus sounded a tone. "If you take the elevator now, you will meet the skycycle at the spin center. Any further delay will delay the mission."

Avram motioned to Celinda. She put her helmet on and stepped into the lock.

As soon as they were underway, with point two four gees pushing them into the backs of their seats, she had a chance to ask questions.

"Just how does a skycycle run away?"

"It can't." Avram's voice was quiet, but had an edge. "Unless someone tampers with the control module."

"They did something to *Dr. Zarkhov*?" She shuddered at the thought of tampering with a cyberbeing that had everyone's safety in its hands.

"No. The control module is below his level, sort of a junior executive. It's like this: We tell *Dr. Zarkhov* what we want to do. *Dr. Zarkhov* works out the mission scenario and feeds the parameters to the control module. The control module sends the signals to gyros, thrusters, and so on. That gives us a little redundancy — even if *Dr. Zarkhov* went down, we could still program the skycycle."

"Oh. *Democritus* runs ours directly. Or we do, manually."

"Yours were made a quarter century ago. We do still have a plug-in manual control module — that's one that takes orders directly from a control stick. If you're really suicidal, you pull out the five cyberlinked control modules and put in one manual module. Then the computer can't control the skycycle, and you can."

"Did Mike do that?"

"He didn't admit it. First he said a thruster accidentally stuck open. Then he wouldn't talk anymore. That was an hour ago."

She looked at the situation display. Peetie and Mike were up to three point six klips and over twelve gigameters distant.

"What about Peetie? I... I don't think he'd hot wire a spacecraft for a joy ride." But she wasn't sure; Peetie was at that age where boys start to change.

"He's along."

"Maybe... maybe because he didn't want Mike to go alone. We really stress the buddy system here. Peetie's a good kid. Really."

Avram patted her leg, which was about the only part of her he could reach from the front seat.

"Maybe that's it then," he offered. But he didn't sound convinced. "Anyway, it's no joy ride anymore. They're out of fuel."

"How do we know?"

"Thirty-five hundred and twenty-eight seconds of thrust at one-tenth gravity — that's all the fuel it had. Also, they aren't going to get anywhere in particular, at least not in this century."

Whoops. "Uh, how are *we* going to get back?"

"We've got an extra tank, behind you. The four of us will go back together on our skycycle. I'll tag the other skycycle and we'll let *Dr. Zarkhov* pick up it later, along with the one your *Democritus* sent out." *Democritus* had sent one without waiting for a crew on the off-chance that he might save a life by acting immediately without a human order, a software fix they called the *Willie mod.*

"Roger."

She looked around. She'd never been so far from the comet before. They seemed fixed in space to her now — too far from anything for their eyes to detect motion. Their skycycle's belly was to the sun, and in its shadow, away from the comet's lights, she could see forever into space. The great Andromeda galaxy was a bright fuzzy lens. Constellations were too crowded with stars to recognize. The steady vibration of the engine lulled her.

"Celinda. We're in suit radio range now. Can you try to call Peter?"

"Huh? Yes. Okay." She cleared her throat. "Peter. Peter, this is Celinda." There was no answer.

"Can this thing go any faster?" she asked, worried again.

"Yes, of course. But it can't *get* us there any faster, if you work in the deceleration."

"Roger."

They passed the auxiliary skycycle. Celinda, in the privacy of her helmet, bit her lip and tried to think of something else.

"Avram, what are you going to do after you guys drop us off at Mars?"

"I'm not really sure. I think this is our last trip as a crew. Mom puts up a brave front, but her heart isn't in things anymore. And Mike, assuming we get him back, well, he doesn't seem to be made for this." There was a long pause. "But *you* do."

It was the nicest thing anyone had ever said to her. She gave Avram a punch on the shoulder.

"What I'd like," Avram continued, "is to take a comet in myself. But I'd need a partner."

Celinda took a deep breath. Was this really happening. She could hear her Mom saying "you're only fifteen!" But if she approached Dad with the argument that the odds were strongly against her ever running into someone like Avram twice in one lifetime, he might tell her to go for it. In fact, maybe that was something he had in mind when he sent her with Avram to get Mike and Peetie, and why Mom acted so funny.

There were going to be changes. Okay. Why not make them all at once? Heart pounding, she chose her words carefully. "My folks want to go back to Earth for a while. Now, if they took Mike with them instead of me..."

The next half hour was one of the shortest and longest in her life.

They had to turn away from the silent skycycle to do the breaking maneuver. *Dr. Zarkhov* held true to his min-time profile, and with over half the skycycle's fuel gone, pushed her in the back with a half gee of deceleration. It was the heaviest she'd ever been outside of the gym, but she almost didn't notice.

Come on, Peetie, she thought. Be there for me. Please be there for me.

Avram worked the rendezvous out to not waste a second. Just as the skycycle matched trajectories Celinda unstrapped and launched herself at the drifting skycycle like a wire-guided missile, trailing her tether.

She could see Mike's arms stuck out in the relaxed position. Peetie's hands seemed to be holding something, but he wasn't moving. His buddy hose was connected to Mike.

"Peetie!" she screamed.

"Celinda," Avram said in a low but still tense voice, "control, now."

He was right. She had to think about first things first. "Roger."

First was landing on the other skycycle. It was dead in space as far as she could tell, drifting like a space boulder. So that's how she'd have to rendezvous. She located the center of tumble, marked it with an eye blink, and headed toward the central truss. Her suit jetted CO_2 until the skycycle stopped drifting across her visor display — a constant angle for intercept. Then she turned herself to land feet first. Looking between her legs, she made sure her feet weren't headed toward anything vital.

She'd landed on a bare section of truss, and absorbed the energy of her jump with bent knees as her boot claws grabbed the truss frame. She looped her tether around the frame so that Avram could pull the two skycycles together.

She could think about Peetie now, and hauled herself around to the top of the skycycle.

There was no sign of violence except that Peetie's comm module was missing from his backpack. She looked at his hands — he had been trying to do something to a comm module — and Mike's was missing from *his* backpack.

"At least you never quit trying," she muttered. Moving like a machine, resigned to the worst, she put her head against Peetie's helmet held her breath and listened.

There was a hiss. That meant his suit was still alive and recycling CO_2 in a minimum power mode. Trembling, she attached her own buddy hose to Peetie's backpack and cranked up the oxygen level. After about twenty seconds of that, she held her helmet hard against his and shouted "Peetie!"

He moved. Dizzy with oxygen and relief, she shook him gently.

He yawned, then recognized where he was. Then his arms were around her and he called her name over and over again between sobs.

There were more groans as Mike started to come around, and a lurch as Avram docked their skycycle on the bottom of Mike's.

"...Dad says we kids never go out alone," Peetie chattered, fully awake now. He was sitting in front of Celinda, doubled up on the skycycle's rear seat, and she had her arms wrapped around him — to keep their helmets in contact so that she could hear him.

Mike was strapped to the cargo rack, sedated. His blue-tinged babble about bad luck and mechanical conspiracies had stopped when Avram had applied a vac-hypo to the gluteus max right through Mike's overclothes and shipsuit. Celinda forgave Avram that bit of brother battering.

"...so," Peetie continued, "I said I had to go with him, or *Democritus* wouldn't let us out. Then I tried to tell him he couldn't take a skycycle. He said to stifle it or he'd turn off my radio. I should have called *Democritus* for help right then, but Mike's bigger than I am and I thought he was kidding.

"I guess he meant it about the radio, because I felt a bump on my back and when we got outside, my radio module was gone. I couldn't get back in without being able to talk to *Democritus*, so I guess I had to go with him.

"When we got to the skycycle, he started pulling modules out of the skycycle and stuck his own in. He did okay driving it at first — real gentle. But it got to be fun, and instead of going right to the Van Doren's spaceship, he started doing acrobatic maneuvers. Then he screwed up and spun us around, got mad and yanked on the controller stick — and it came off. He tried to fix it by sticking things in the hole left when the stick broke, and we kept going faster. I was getting real scared. I thought if I could just stop Mike from doing crazy things, someone could catch us, so I turned down his oxygen when he wasn't looking.

"I tried to take his radio module and put it in my suit so I could call, but I couldn't see my back, or the module wasn't the same kind, or something. Then the skycycle ran out of fuel and starting running out of power too. Mike's backpack power was really low, so I used my buddy connector, but to keep him out, I had to turn my oxygen down, too. So I got tired, too and fell asleep trying to get power from my wrist light to Mike's comm module. That's when you found me, Ceecie. Sorry."

It didn't even occur to Celinda to object to the nickname, or to anticipate that her reaction to his apology would cause Peetie to refer to her as 'my Boa Consister' from then on.

"Are you all right, Ceecie?" her husband asked as her ghosts faded.

Yes, she was all right, but it felt as good as ever to be the object of his concern. She wiped a tear from her face, and looked up into his strong quiet face. She'd gotten used to the grayness in his temples, but, impishly, she pinched a love handle. They both needed more time in the gym.

"I was just feeling a little nostalgic — remembering when Dad made this for us." She touched the sliced-off face from the corner stone of three children's castle in the sky. It now bore tons of memories instead of tons of rock.

"I know it seems silly, but I feel whole again, every time I touch it. Mom, Dad, Willie, and Peetie are all there for me again, inside. I mean it's all gone. But it's all here, too. Dad gave me something I could touch."

"Doesn't seem silly at all, love. Say, speaking of family, Mike sent a hologram from LA. The *Aliens* actually sold something, got into the top fifty, and his share of the royalties might be enough to qualify him and Oona to move up from their dole-burg and get a repro permit. Would you believe he had two hundred *thousand* people spread out in front of his band! Put it on the screen, *Uhura*."

A sea of faces appeared on the screen above packing boxes. Celinda shivered and remembered that the total human population was approaching twenty billion. Twenty people at a vector planning conference every decade or so was her idea of a big crowd.

"What a strange world. So I might actually get to be an aunt before I'm a grandmother!"

"If Peter and Lisa haven't already done *that* for you."

Celinda smiled. Peetie and his wife had a twelve year drop into New Mars, as of their last holo. That was plenty of time to do something, and all their news was four point three years old.

She grinned. "At least their news is comprehensible!" She touched her freshly cleaned piece of comet, and traced P. I. over Peetie's initials. Peetie had carved them in with the others when Dad made the table as a wedding present. *Love, Sis*, she thought. Then she wiped off the top again, hard, as if she could polish off the protective film and get right down to the rock.

"Mom!" Billy called out from behind the pile of boxes in his room. "Cilly and I are not virtual bodlinking. We're just friends. So you can valve-off that talk about being a grandmother, okay?"

AFTERWORD — COMET GYPSIES

MY MODEST CONTRIBUTION to making a new Martian atmosphere has been a variant on the idea of using Kuiper belt objects for raw material. A small army of (perhaps self-replicating) robots, with a human overseer or two, would be put on them during the decades-long fall into the inner solar system. En route, the robots refine these comets into their constituent volatiles and store them as mountains of gravel-sized ice grains.

Instead of crashing everything directly onto Mars, as the refined comet approaches, the useful stuff is diverted toward Mars, dispersed and slowed by solar light pressure. On entry, the incoming mass produces a large-scale meteor shower which doesn't reach the ground. The slag and the robots continue around the Sun (perhaps with a little delta V so it doesn't take decades to get back out again, and the robots get off and pick up the next comet. This, I realize, lacks the drama of pulverizing the planet with impacts, but is, I think, a more controllable and predictable way to go. At any rate, that idea is the basis for "Comet Gypsies," about a family overseeing the refining of such an inbound comet.

In Martyn Fogg's book, *Terraforming* I find that Freeman Dyson has calculated that Saturn's moon Enceladus has sufficient mass for the project, about 6.5 E19 kg. As a typical virgin comet might have a mass of 3.2 E 16 kg, so a couple thousand of them should do, maybe 20,000 if the ammonia content is low. Dyson was thinking in terms of 13,000 years, with the incoming mass providing an equivalent of 9% of Martian insolation during that time.

I would be a little less patient, using a much higher mass flow with solar braking to cut down entry heating, aiming the mass flow toward the poles, and using the reentry heat to help keep the newly deposited atmosphere from condensing there. Half of the glowing meteors' energy is radiated directly away to space, and half or more of what's left would likely be reflected by clouds — which is a good thing, because otherwise Mars might get too hot.

It is one of those fascinating systems things that the limiting concern on how fast we could give Mars a breathable atmosphere is the accretional heating — the propulsion and industrial matters seem almost trivial by robotic manufacturing standards! If we could stand to double Martian heat input (equivalent to moving Mars into Earth's orbit), I think the job could be done in about 200 years, with settlement activities in the equatorial regions starting much earlier.

My end product is a 12% O_2, 88% N_2 atmosphere 150% the total mass of Earth's, 2.6 times the column mass, about twice the surface pressure/density with a tropopause at about 40 km altitude and an effective temp of about 200 K, with an average lapse rate of about 2.5 K/km to the surface. I preferred to achieve the desired surface temperature with a thicker atmosphere rather than playing with the CO_2 and other greenhouse gas percentages. I imagine that actively managed biological and physical control systems will be needed for some time to keep it that way, but that some degree of stability will be achieved in the long run.

The stability of a long term home is one of those human needs that most people have had to learn to do without, though every now and then you read about someone who was born and died in the same house. Between 1969 and 1976, I moved twelve times, nine of those being Air Force related and the rest due to changes in personal circumstances. While there's some stress in each change, after a while, you began to get numb.

But the place where you grow up is special, and, even many years later when you go through the town where you were born, you might take time to at least drive by and remember.

The place where Celinda grew up was doomed; by the end of the story, there is literally no *there* there anymore. Its secrets and trage-dies live on only in her memories and those of her family. But some sixty of seventy percent of it does become part of the atmosphere of Mars, and when she visits there, perhaps she will take some comfort in the knowledge that some of those trillions of atoms she breathes in and out were once the caves, spires, playgrounds, and graveyard of her homeworld.

MONSTERS BELOW

"**N**OT VERY PRETTY, were they?"

Hive-Lord Althor was not feeling in a judgmental mood. Back in normal gravity after a few turns on the high gravity world below them, he flexed his tentacles and bounced on his footpad with renewed vigor. What could be ugly when he felt this way?

Oh, Eldest Daughter's observation was right by conventional standards; from what pictures they could find, the first people were bags of soft flesh hanging from a frame like a meat-rack. But to Althor, there was a certain *functional* aesthetic involved, the form and function kind of thing. "Perhaps, but for what they were and where they lived..."

Low tones came back, though from a respectful posture.

"Bone cross section too large, too strongly built, they were too short for this horizon and this gravity. Hive-Father, they were not as ugly for this world as they would be on ours, but still, I can't model their evolution here."

Althor's tentacles drooped. "Evolution can do many surprising things. They came in two genders, but in almost equal proportions. We have some sea worms like that, but..."

"Yes, Hive-Father. Look, this world is remarkably clean given the length of time it was inhabited. Primitives aren't that clean. But right from the start, the first ones apparently didn't die very often, didn't make stone tools, didn't leave refuse piles about."

Althor put out some medium frequency tones, his people's equivalent of "I know, I know."

But Eldest Daughter was not through. "We have sonic imagers, micro-subsurface samplers, high-energy photon scatter pattern tomography, and over thirty million artificial intelligences going over every part of this world that hasn't been overrun with lava or blasted by asteroids in the last three billion revolutions. From all that we have only eight fossilized partial skeletons, three vehicles and parts of a fourth, a few dozen diamond covered picture pins. And..."

"They cleaned up after themselves, then. We do much the same."

"But that was a lesson learned only after thousands of generations."

"Maybe they learned it faster."

"Eldest Daughter, we have only tasted a drop from an ocean. Look at these huge volcanic remains; the entire surface of the planet may have been resurfaced since intelligence evolved. Your answers may lie buried far beneath ancient lava, halfway to the core and melted away." He stabbed a tentacle down.

Eldest Daughter spread tentacles in a gesture of calm that was also a contradiction to Hive-Father's gesture, but not an obvious one. "The resurfacing has not been so rapid, and there are many caves, ancient lava tubes that were never filled in because the wet periods were so short. Something may have gone in one of those and been preserved, sealed away by subsequent flows."

"Oh, perhaps."

"I have found such a tube and mean to explore it."

Eldest Father's posture changed from haughtiness to protectiveness, and he reached his tentacles toward her ever so slightly. "Yourself? That could be dangerous..."

"Nothing dangerous lives down there anymore."

"Look around you; the rock still lives."

A LIFE ON MARS

"**P**ETE, THERE'S A priority message from Jovis Tholus University Hospital, your personal code. A Dr. Baklinova." There was a hint of urgency in Waldo's otherwise calm, somewhat Hitchcockian voice — a slight increase in pace, perhaps more emphasis on the higher harmonics? Whatever it was, the programmer's magic worked; I could sense the tension the computer personality tried to convey.

"Hold it for a moment." There was only one person on Mars this call could be about, and I wasn't ready to deal with it cold. My ex, Jeanette, had left us for Mars back in 2046, literally without saying goodbye until she was on the transport. Then, April and I were so much surplus baggage. Now, apparently, she was in some kind of medical trouble.

I looked out the window. It was almost eight in the evening, universal time, and there were only a few lights on the eastern wall of the South Trench, reflected in the swimmer-rippled waters of the central park lake. Mars sat maybe ten degrees over the eastern wall, easily bright enough to see through the moonglass of the arched trench roof despite my office lights. The red planet was approaching opposition, just over sixty million kilometers away-about as near as anything major gets to anything else in the solar system. But an eternity away in my personal life.

My desk sat in front of me filled with papers, real ones scattered over the virtual ones in the desktop screen. Work to me, life itself to my students. Sorry, kids, something's come up... "Put it on the north wall screen," I told Waldo.

I tried to do something with a student's asteroid habitat design while light crawled to Mars and back. About nine minutes later, the view of Earth faded to white and my caller faded in.

Dr. Baklinova was nowhere to be seen. It was Jeanette. I didn't recognize her at first; she was in some kind of hospital bed, her head was immobilized, shaved, and there was a bandage over her right eye. Her face was bruised, mottled black blue and yellow. The rest of her was covered.

"Hello, Pete." Her voice was not much more than a whisper. "Pete, there was a quake, a cave in and I got hurt pretty bad. Among other things, I need a lung. They tell me I can't tolerate the stuff they use to make non-matching transplants, and I won't last long enough to grow a new one. But April is a tissue match; one of her lungs would work. Sorry to be so direct. Not much strength. Not much time. They're going to try to keep me going until you get here. Please." She opened her mouth as if to say something more, then closed it.

The view switched to an office with a sturdy woman in a blue shirt sitting behind a desk.

"Hello, Mr. Nelson, I'm Dr. Lada Baklinova at Jovis Tholus University hospital." Russian, I thought, from the name and the accent. "Your wife..."

"I'm not married to her anymore," I said automatically, then remembered the time lag. Sixty-four million kilometers away, a little over two hundred seconds at 300,000 kilometers per second. Three and a half minutes, say. The correction would likely arrive after Baklinova had signed off.

"...and insisted on making the appeal herself. You are probably wondering why we can't do a transplant from someone here. Your wife, unfortunately, is among the two or three percent of the population who have a strong toxic reaction to the drugs we need for that. There are facilities on Earth that might be able to handle the reaction, but here, it would be fatal. We do not have any donors close enough to do it without those drugs. But your daughter, April, would be match.

"However the odds of Mrs. Nelson surviving on full life support until a donor arrives are not very good, even at a reduced metabolic rate, there's about an even chance that she will die in seventy hours, maybe one chance in ten of surviving a week. Less than one in a hundred of surviving long enough for the next scheduled space transport. We will not give up, of course, and if you decide to come, we will do what we can to increase those odds, but it would be a big surprise if she lasted. I am very sorry, about your wife but I thought it would be best if you know the truth. Baklinova Out."

"She's not my wife!" I yelled.

"Pete...?" Waldo asked.

Waldo has standing orders to put any emotional outbursts on my part on ten second delay.

"Right, Waldo, don't send that."

"The sentence 'She's not my wife' has been deleted."

The view switched back to Jeanette.

We were near opposition — Mars, Earth and Sun nearly lined up. A Monarch-class ion liner could get there in six weeks and an IPA cutter could... I didn't know what the current record was.

Please begin your response appeared along the bottom of the now-frozen screen.

Not yet. I had to think.

♂ ♂ ♂

Memories. She'd been a bright young woman when we married, a few years younger than me, with long straight brown hair and a sharp, almost elfin kind of face. I'd kept her picture on my desk, maybe longer than I should have.

Moonlit walks on campus. Riverbanking. Learning about love together. Coping with a child and careers that kept each of us traveling. Her ultimatum that led to my quitting the engineering corps and joining the University faculty. Setting up the household at Coriolis Crater. April's first day at school in the last quarter of ninety-five. Seven years ago, but some days it seemed like we'd just gotten here.

♂ ♂ ♂

The time delay between planets encourages a certain lack of concentration — I'd been musing for two minutes. Back to the present, Pete — time to say something. What? *Gee that's too bad, we had some nice times. I'll have April send a get well message.*

I owed that woman nothing anymore. Nothing.

But there was a challenge in this and my mind had already started making calculations. My friend and colleague, Ahmed Fahsi, ran the spaceflight research station at Martinez Crater and was also its chief engineer. The Cislunar Republic's version of Sergei Korolev, Werner Von Braun, or Kelly Johnson, his beamriders hadn't been well received in the traditional, self-contained spacecraft world, and he was looking for publicity. But he had completed one ship — the *Edmund Halley* — that had performed several spectacular missions, including a comet rendezvous.

It could do, what, three or four gravities? I could probably ignore solar gravity... allow ten million kilometers for acceleration and deceleration... cruise for fifty kiloseconds at 1000 km per second... 40 kiloseconds at 25 meters per second... Jupiter gravity... survive that lying down... It might take a day and a half and Jeanette might last a couple of days on the machine... No, that was ridiculous. Or was it?

This would be a good excuse for Ahmed to show the Solar System what his stuff could do. He might go for it. He just might.

The engineer in me was at war with the abused ex-husband. And the engineer was winning. Something between twenty and forty hours might actually be possible.

The "Please begin your response" line started flashing. The doctor probably needed to put her to sleep, so she'll last longer. Other people need to use the circuits. I'd better say something.

"I'm really sorry you got hurt, Jeanette. This is pretty sudden, I haven't had a chance to think anything through. April's at school — drill team practice tonight — and..."

What if April said 'yes?' What would you do then, Pete, you idiot?

"...you're a tough lady, so I think you have as good a chance as anyone to pull through this. Maybe there's something we can do. I'll send another message tonight with April. Uh... Peter Nelson out."

The screen cleared, replaced by the cool blue seas and swirling clouds of Earth again, but I couldn't see it. What I saw was a surgeon's laser plunging into my innocent daughter's chest.

"Waldo, check the medical data they dumped. Just how much lung capacity does Jeanette have left?"

The answer was immediate. "None."

What had that doctor said? Full life support? She'd meant it. "But how?"

"Pulmonary edema when her suit was breached," Waldo answered. "There was some function in the left lung for a day or so, but that's gone now. She's being maintained artificially. The heart's gone too, but that prosthesis is fairly standard, even on Mars. Lungs are much more difficult."

"No heart? No lungs? How long can she last?"

"They removed the dead tissue and started budding a new left lung in the chest cavity. But that will take several months to come on line. The longevity record for being on combined heart-lung machines is about eight weeks, and that was achieved by someone who was in much better shape otherwise. A high rate of micro-clotting due to the enormous exposure to foreign material and capillary fouling are the main problems. This case yields a fifty percent survival time of fifty-eight hours, with a decline to one percent at three hundred eleven hours."

"Got it." Pretty much the same numbers the doctor had. "Why do they need a tissue match? Can't they just reprogram the immune system or something?"

"Do you want the long or the short answer?"

I'd taught Waldo to ask that. One gets busy at times.

"The short one for now."

"They would need to reprogram every cell in the donor organ or in the recipient body. They aren't there yet."

I thought furiously. To delay anything would be tantamount to a decision not to help, and I wasn't ready to decide that yet. I had to proceed as if April was going to donate and we were going to Mars. If we weren't... well, that was the decision I could make at the last moment. I was just preserving my options, that's all. Jeanette got herself into that mess and just maybe she would have to pay the price instead of cutting up our kid to get out of it.

Jeanette. For better or worse, by some primordial law of imprinting, I still felt responsible for her. But the decision was not mine. I could not tell April to do this. But I would ask.

I didn't want this. I really didn't.

♂ ♂ ♂

Memories came flooding back again.

For some reason, I'd said yes to a consulting job in Kurdistan in eighty-six. We'd fabricated a dam liner on the moon to help the Kurds control a river without destroying its flood plain. It weighed thirty thousand tons and with a terminal velocity of fifty meters per second, it had to fall in exactly the right place, its impact cushioned by thirteen hundred computer controlled CO jets. Then we finished molding it to the terrain with a cloud of superheated steam. We were little a behind schedule but perfect execution was worth the delay. I'd been focused on that to the exclusion of everything else for three months and felt ready to celebrate the achievement.

But, in a matter of hours, my elation became loss and despair. They'd found the microbe colonies in the roots of Olympus Mons and there was a transport due out that week. Jeanette left April with her sister and got on it; planets don't wait. She actually called me from the ship, outbound — *fait accompli.*

Then there was the dragging out of it all. There'd been nothing final in her departure message, and she'd left April and many personal things as if she'd intended to return some day. It was the months of uncertainty that had hurt as much as anything else.

Messages went back and forth every day for a while. Then every week. There was a ship scheduled to leave Mars six months after she arrived — would she be done by then? Maybe. Another ship six weeks later. She promised to be on that one, but changed her mind. I got that message after it had left Phobos. Was I still married? What was going on? The calls came every week, then every month, then a year.

I remembered very clearly the last time I'd said "I love you" to her — I'd been crying then, too. That had been five years ago. Kids are more adaptable; April Jeanne had stopped asking "When is Mommy coming home?" long before that.

Tamika had moved in with us a year or so after that — no contract, no guarantees; she had just emigrated from Hawaii and latched onto us like one atom of hydrogen latches onto another in need of a complete electron shell. Some semblance of a family had begun to form again.

The official divorce had been in ninety-one, with her signature faxed from three kilometers underground somewhere in Tharsis; she'd been interviewed there on that Astrographic special about the microworms, apparently unaffected by anything in her personal life.

Then, three years ago, Jeanette began talking about bringing April to Mars. I'd said 'no,' and things had gotten testy.

♂ ♂ ♂

"Waldo, would you explain the situation to the school officials? I'll be there to talk to April in about ten minutes. And see if you can find Ahmed Fahsi and have him call me on the way."

I looked out at my balcony. As an assistant professor, I'd earned an inner office only three stories up, and, in the old days, would have jumped to the sidewalk below without a second thought. But a month ago some idiot Earth tourist kid had broken a leg and injured a pedestrian trying that without knowing how, and the muni council, in a fit of paternalism, had forbidden jumping to the street from the third floor up. So I had to take the interior pole, about ten doors north of my office.

My mind clamped onto ordinary things like a vise, as if to keep itself off the upcoming conversation with April: the smoothness of the pole on my hand as I braked my descent; the smell of the giant roses along the path to the school.

As I passed the athletic clearing, a moonball bounced in front of me. I grabbed it automatically and threw it back up at a young man gliding back to the turf on a slow lunar trajectory, his skin bare glistening with sweat and eyes bright with excitement. He was immediately tackled by an equally bare girl and the ball went flying away into a knot of youngsters.

How bad a scar would the operation leave on April? They wanted a lung. It would be a huge incision, it would have to be. What kind of sacrifice was I asking her to make — having scars on the chest is okay for guys, a macho thing. But for girls, it could be a disfigurement. She was just beginning to develop and deathly proud of it. No, I was back in my childhood again; they could fix a surgical scar now, generate fresh skin. In a few months she wouldn't be able to find it.

"Pete, Ahmed." His voice came in on my ear piece. I didn't look at my wrist for a picture — I knew what Ahmed looked like — an almost two meter bear of a man, bald as a cue ball, sporting the gentle brown tan he was born with. "I got your message about Jeanette. I have bad news, I'm afraid."

I stumbled and almost did a flip and had to rotate my arms wildly to get a foot down for the next stride. "Ahmed, Pete. Let's have it."

"The *Edmund Halley* left for Ceres thirteen hours ago. She hasn't finished acceleration, but I can't get her back. You know how it works."

I knew. Ahmed's ships have to be pushed by a mass beam — their main engines stay on the moon, and wait for them at their destination. That's why they can go so fast; they don't have to carry their reaction mass. But it also means a certain lack of flexibility.

"Damn! Any idea of what the Coriolis launch track could give an IPA ship, with a full load for post launch acceleration?" The Interplanetary Authority had the fastest high-gee ships in the solar system, next to the *Edmund Halley* .

I had a mental picture of Ahmed shrugging his shoulders. "A hydrogen-propellant nuclear thermal IPA cutter can fly with a mass ratio of twenty — that means do about three times their exhaust velocity, and their exhaust velocity was about of eleven kilometers per second — now add six for the maximum launch track boost and you should get maybe thirty six kilometers per second total delta vee? Eighteen up, eighteen down. But it is not pointed the right direction. If you wait for the Moon to come around in two weeks, you do not get there much sooner than an ion liner anyway."

That should have been just fine. I didn't really want to go anyway. Options closed, no guilt, okay?

Not okay.

"Ahmed, you've got some other things in work, don't you, and some experimental stuff from before the *Halley*?"

"May Allah be praised." It was Ahmed's habit to say this quickly and softly and it came out sounding something like "mahlabraced," the way someone born in a Christian culture might say "Geez." It was a relic of a his past; we shared that — having previous lives. "Just what kind of risk are you willing to take?" he added.

"Not willing, just considering at this point. But if April says yes, that would mean she's willing to undergo a major operation and live on one lung for a while. So I'm willing to consider risk on that level. What are the options?"

"Silence.

"Ahmed?"

"You have posed an interesting problem. Come over here ready to go immediately and I will explain your options then."

"How...?"

"I do not know fully myself, yet. But where there is such a will, surely a way can be found. I will tell you now that I have two fully functional reflector rings in the yard, but without very much ship around either of them. What I can do with them I cannot say yet. But time is very short, so you make your preparations and come as if I already have an answer, all right?"

"Bless you Ahmed, I haven't asked April yet. She'll likely say 'no way.'"

"April is a remarkable young woman, Pete. She visited my field several times with her classmates, and I think she has more... I do not know the word... more *jets* in her than all of them. True, she may say 'no.' But I will wait for you nevertheless. Good luck and out."

My legs were on autopilot, and as my talk with Ahmed finished, I arrived in a playground full of laughing children in blue jumpsuits, milling around in no detectable order. The South Trench Bluebirds, I recalled, whose practice must be over. April was a raven haired pixie with double pigtails and a white shell necklace — lunar snail shells left by lunar snails from the Central Parks that had moved onto bigger and better things — escargot at Duluth's restaurant, for instance. April collected them for Marie Duluth, and got to keep the shells in payment. I scanned the kids.

But I recognized Tamika's willowy figure first, next to a tall birch silhouetted in the school's soft yard light and then April next to her. Complications. I owed Tamika whatever emotional stability I'd gained in the last five years and I was proposing going to Mars to save her predecessor. How would she react to a mission to save her predecessor? Jeanette might ask us to stay. I had a daughter with her and so much history together... it had been my greatest wish that everything that had happened could go away and I could have my family back again. Hope had died hard; Tamika knew that.

I loped toward them with ten-meter strides and caught the trunk of the birch with my left hand to help bring myself to a dignified halt.

Tamika's Eurasian features were calm but serious as she urged April toward me. April leaped the last few meters between us, into my arms.

"Tammy told me Mom's hurt bad!"

I looked at Tamika.

"I called Waldo," she said. "I haven't told her everything."

"Yes," I said. I hadn't thought of telling him not to tell her. This was going to be tough on her, I thought, and unavoidable, now. "Let's sit down somewhere."

There was a bench near the school entrance, an ordinary gray sintered moondust bench, with kids' initials carved in it. The other kids were melting away, leaving us alone.

Where to start? "April, your mother got hurt in a cave-in and needs a lung transplant within a few days if she is going to live."

"She might die? You want to say goodbye before she has the operation?"

I shook my head. "They don't have any appropriate donors on Mars, or anywhere nearby. Your blood and tissue are the right type — they want you to be the donor."

"Me?" Her eyes went wide and her mouth formed a huge "O" as the implications set in. April had perfect teeth. I tried to remember the last time we'd stuck a dental examiner in her mouth — should do that every month, but things get busy — if it came to a custody fight, would that count against me? April was staring at me — there'd been a question mark at the end of that "Me?"

"You," I said.

"But we're here and Mars is there!" April looked up in the sky in the right direction, bless her, and, in a blink, pointed to the right bright red star. I had to smile. What a kid!

"Ahmed might be able to get us there in time."

It was Tamika's turn to get wide-eyed. "This is possible?"

"He's not sure, but he didn't say 'no' right away. If April says 'yes,' we're to pack and get over there right away. Mars is setting, and it has to be above the horizon for his thing to work."

"You still love Mom a little, don't you Dad?" April asked.

"April, there are still some things that you're a little too young…"

"Nuts. I'll bet you don't even know that I know why my name is April when I was born in January?"

"April!"

Tamika giggled.

"Look," I said. "You can't be that close to someone and not have feelings, whatever they are. But my feelings aren't so important now; it's your lung. The question is, are you willing to donate a lung to save someone's life?"

April looked down at her chest, then drew a line with her finger from her collar bone down over her right breast to the bottom of her rib cage. Her fingernail left a thin crease in the blue fabric. She looked up at me, scared. "Either that or Mom dies, huh?"

I shut my eyes. No. Yes. "April, I don't know how they do operations like that but they can probably repair anything they do in a couple of months or so."

Tamika put a hand on my shoulder. "I think what they used to do is to split the breast bone, not the breast, then pull the rib cage back, and take it out that way. But now, I think they can go in under the rib cage, through the diaphragm, with all sorts of special tools. Still, for a lung, I think it would have to be a big incision."

April looked at her, then back at her chest and drew another line below her rib cage. Then she looked at Tamika again.

"Will it hurt?"

"Yes," Tamika said, "but not until after the operation. They'll put you to sleep for the operation itself. They will have pills to help you endure the pain afterward."

It dawned on me that Tamika was speaking in favor of saving the life of the woman who was still her rival in my affections, no matter how much I tried to deny it.

"Another ethics lesson?" April asked.

"Yes," Tamika said at once, answering both April's question and mine.

"What goes in there if they take the lung out?" April pointed to her chest.

Waldo found out. They use a degradable air jell bag that serves as a scaffold and then dissolves away as the new lung grows in its place.

April asked more questions and pretty soon we all had a good picture of what was involved. Finally, April nodded her head with an expression so serious that only children on the verge of adolescence can manage it.

"Cool. I can deal with it. Do I get to go to Mars? Or just my lung?"

Tamika smiled. "The less time a donated organ spends out of a body, the better."

"Can I keep the scar, Dad? That would be *really* gross. The kids would *stare*. They'd be vacuum boiled! Can I keep the scar, huh?"

People who think they understand kids should have one. I put an arm around mine and smiled.

"Look, there's no guarantee that we can get to Mars in time. But we have to play it as if we could, so we're going home to grab a change of clothes and an overnight kit. Everything else we need we'll get when and if we get to Mars. Then we're going to Ahmed Fahsi's launch site and — "

"Beamriders! We're going to get to go on a beamrider!"

"Maybe, April. Maybe."

♂ ♂ ♂

"Maybe, Pete."

We were in spacesuits with duffel bags on the spotless lunar concrete of the experimental rocket base. Mars hung red and brilliant about ten degrees above the west horizon, in Sagittarius. The Milky Way outlined the distant western ring wall.

"This is the *Korolev*, or it will be when we finish it. It looks a bit, how would you say it, ramshackle now. But it is more than strong enough. Stronger, really, without all the pretty stuff." 'This' looked something like an outsized lunar wire-basket wheel without a hub. It was at least fifty meters from center to edge and lay on its side, held off the regolith by three man-sized posts. The lattice frame enclosed an incomplete ten-meter-long sausage-shaped cabin — the surface of this section was infested by spider-like robots going about various tasks. Cables and pipes ran around in open conduit on the outside perimeter of the ring, occasionally intersecting pairs of spherical tanks. The conduit terminated diametrically across from the cabin among some dark gray tanks with radiation warning symbols all over them. It looked very much like a work in progress.

"Is that really enough? What if there's a radiation storm?" The mass of a big liner and its life support system can come in handy at times.

"There is a solar storm in progress, as it happens, but the drive's magnetic field will protect you from that. For a day or two of life support, you do not need the whole hull."

A day or two. The implications of setting a record like that started to sink in. It would be revolutionary and not everyone liked revolutions, especially unplanned revolutions.

Tamika and April skipped over to it in their vacuum suits, kicking up small sprays of dust as they went. I stayed back with Ahmed.

"We just brought her down from a ten-day hour hover test. She flies fine, Pete. The robots — they are making some final life support arrangements."

"Where's the door?" April's asked, from the ship.

Ahmed's face was unreadable for the reflected stars, but one can do an adequate shrug in a vacuum suit. "There is not time for everything. Plates on each end are removable from the inside if you depressurize first. You'll have vacuum tape to seal it from the inside."

No. There was no way I was going to go through with this. Not this way. "Ahmed..." I began to say no, but what I heard myself saying instead was, "...just in case we are crazy enough to do this, how long to Phobos?"

Ahmed waved a hand at an innocent-looking dome near the corner of the space port. "The mass accelerator could push a complete ship at three gravities. Like that," he gestured to the skeletal, partly finished ship. "It has so little mass, I could push you at up to five gravities."

Five gravities? I remembered my calculation. I couldn't concentrate well enough to do another one, but it seemed that five gravities would get us there in less than a day. This didn't seem real. Interplanetary journeys took months — well, weeks if you were really in a hurry. Five gravities...?

"How far can you push us?" April asked. "Can you hit the ship with the beam all the way to Mars?"

"Aha!" Ahmed said, grinning. He produced a small transparent bag full of what looked to be dust, took a handful and tossed it high into the lunar night. "Watch this!" He pointed a small rod in the direction of the dust that emitted nothing that I could see. But the dust particles began to twinkle furiously as they fell, forming a fuzzy solid cylinder with its axis directed toward Ahmed's rod.

"Fairy dust?" April squealed. "You have *fairy dust!?*"

"Fairy dust if you like, little one. The particles I push the ship with are trying to push themselves toward the center of this ultraviolet beam with little flashes of light of their own. If I could give them more time, they would do so. With these, I can push you as far as I want — maybe to Alpha Centauri if I can shoot the particles fast enough! But you would have to slow down at the other end and I don't have a base there..." He grinned. "...yet. But Mars is no problem."

"Five gees is thirty times April's normal weight!" Tamika said.

"How would I fly it?" I asked.

Ahmed raised a hand. "Oh, one at a time, please! Now — I can adjust the flotation beds I have on hand to fit your vacuum suits in a few minutes." He pointed toward some coffin shaped objects. "Immersed at neutral buoyancy, you will not feel so much acceleration. Everything is ready; I only need to make a rough mold of your form so we do not use too much flotation oil and have so much extra mass that our acceleration is compromised. You cannot fly the ship — there are no manual controls yet. The computers will control everything — but do not worry, they are five times redundant."

I stared at the ramshackle ring of lattice, pipes, boxes and cylinders. I did not need to take this chance. I didn't owe her anything. "This is looking a little like pushing the limit to me, Ahmed, I might risk it myself, but with a twelve-year-old..."

"Dad..."

Ahmed cleared his throat. "Cabin conditions will be very primitive, but it would only be for a few hours." He seemed to be trying to sell me on it. He'd known Jeanette, of course; the Moon was still a small place. Was he helping her as much as me? We never really know how others view a split up; maybe he thought it was my fault. Or maybe he... none of my business, really.

"I'm tight, Dad," April said. "I can handle it."

I looked at Tamika. She looked at me. Ahmed looked at his wrist comp.

"Compared to the value of the experience, the risk is small," Tamika said. "Not many people have the opportunity to do such a deed."

Over the last two years, I had come to rely on her for such judgments. My mind was numb.

I thought of being sealed in that thin-walled tomb. Risk. Speed. Experience. Letting go. I nodded. A life was at stake, one that I had tried to write out of my universe but here it came calling back like some kind of ghoul for the unfinished business that was our daughter. Should what I felt be the controlling consideration? Or was this fate pounding at the door?

There seemed nothing I could do but nod and as I did my stomach became tight as a drum. It wasn't a well-reasoned decision. Maybe I would get away with it.

"Very well," said Ahmed "Allah be with you." He said that slowly, almost like a prayer.

♂ ♂ ♂

The next hour was blur that ended with April and me floating in our acceleration beds in the cabin of the skeletal spacecraft — a very functional looking control room with racks of equipment, a rat's nest of cabling, and bare titanium lattice girders wherever there weren't screens. Ahmed had stuck standard one-meter screens every which way to the point where the hull looked mostly transparent. The one just over my feet showed Mars, sinking toward the lunar horizon. We would have to complete our acceleration before it came between us and Ahmed's drive projectors.

Incongruously, one screen overhead showed the *Korolev* on its pad as seen from Ahmed's control center at the edge of the field. It looked more ramshackle than ever.

Just inside the one true opening of our cabin, a stick-man robot under the *Korolev*'s control held a panel that would function as our "door." As a safety measure, we would wait until achieving lunar escape velocity before closing it and pressurizing the cabin. Our "coffins" sat on a floor bare except for a pair of trunks of life support gear. One would give us our air, the toilet was in the other. We could unpack that once the cabin was sealed.

"Are you ready, April?"

"Sure, Dad." There was tension in that voice. A hell of a lot of tension.

"Ready here, Ahmed."

"Raise the ship," Ahmed told his comp.

"The instruction has been countermanded," the soft, female, voice of the control center's AI declared. "Port Captain Kelly wishes to speak with whoever is in charge of this flight."

Ahmed groaned. "This is my launch, Kelly."

"*Korolev*, put Kelly and Ahmed on the front screen," I said. Mars vanished.

Bart Kelly, a large muscular man with curly black hair, came on screen. I knew him from somewhere.

"We can't allow this, Ahmed."

"There are extraordinary circumstances, Bart. Any delay at all may cost a life."

"Which I understand may very well be lost anyway. I wouldn't want to lose other lives on the chance. Fahsi, this isn't the time or the way to be setting any Moon-Mars speed records. Give it up."

"What," Ahmed said between nearly clenched teeth, "do we have to do to satisfy you? The vehicle is space worthy — it has completed ten times the length of the journey in hover tests. I have enough redundancy for computer piloting."

Kelly smiled with teeth showing. "There are Cislunar Republic resources involved here and a judgment call to make which is not yours alone."

"Very well. What do we have to do?"

"Comply with the provisions of the Cislunar Space Navigation Protocol."

Ahmed looked like he was about to explode. I didn't know Kelly, but thought a diversion was in order. "Pete Nelson here. Captain Kelly, I thought we were in compliance. What is your objection?"

"I don't have time to go through the details, Mr. Nelson. My autosec can arrange an appointment with our legal staff."

I smelled a rat. A specific problem can be dealt with and this guy was doing everything he could not to specify — it seemed a delay tactic. Whose ax was Kelly grinding?

"We'll correct whatever might be wrong and file again."

"That's your privilege, but I just don't think it's going to work. In my humble opinion, this is just too risky. Kelly out."

Finally I placed the face. "Ahmed, I think Kelly used to fly L1 shuttles."

"Of course he did. And now he's stuck playing port captain waiting for a shift leader's berth on a deep space ion liner." Ahmed looked furious. "Spacetrans! —and they do not want to replace their ion rockets! And the space crews — you need three times as many people to run an ion rocket liner as one of my design; they don't want to see that number go down. I bet someone in Spacetrans promised him a berth if he keeps us here. This demonstration would be broadcast all over the solar system — and they do not want to see that just yet! You may as well come back to the control center. We have, what, maybe an hour to figure this out."

To get Ahmed to *really* do something, tell him it can't be done. April and I got up, clambered out of the *Korolev* and headed for the control center.

Ahmed, Tamika, and I each had a terminal and a section of the Protocol to study. Ahmed looked like he could take a scimitar to someone's neck. Tamika's slick little page cut generally didn't need maintenance — but now she combed it furiously with her hand. God knows what I looked like.

"Why don't we just go anyway?" April wanted to know. "You know, like civil disobedience."

Ahmed turned toward her, and waved a hand. "Even though I built it, this facility does not belong to me; I just get to run it. I must obey the law or someone else will take my work."

"Why won't the vac-boiled idiots let us go?"

"Because we are a threat to someone."

"But that's not ethical either, is it Tamika?"

Tamika clapped her hands. "No, it's not, nor can it be legal. Look, guys, I think we're working the problem from the wrong end. Kelly may not have to give *us* a reason to bar our departure, but he certainly had to give one to the Port computer! Ahmed, can you find out what it was?"

He shook his head. "I do not have the authority..."

Authority. Jeanette's cousin, Tad Reynolds. I knew him only slightly, but he ran the Cislunar Republic's public service corps. He could probably care less about me now, but in this case...

"I know someone who does," I said.

It took Ahmed's AI a couple of minutes to find him and put him on. Tad had a boyish shock of light brown hair that made him look more 30-something than the 50-something I knew him to be. After I explained the situation, he pursed his lips, looked somewhere in his office, and did something I couldn't see with his hands.

"The human control provisions of Interplanetary Association Treaty," Tad said after a moment.

"But I'm a fully qualified pilot and April will be on board, too!" I was confused. Human control: a face-saving issue in the carefully negotiated detente between the United Nations of Earth and the Cislunar Republic thirty years ago — the people at the bottom of the Terrestrial gravity well wanted someone to blame if things fell on them, and the negotiators felt they had to allow some pretext of moral justification for the U.N.'s unsuccessful power play. Human control was a formality these days — everything smart enough to know it existed had human control burned into it.

"According to the rules, April does not qualify as a redundant human control."

"But kids her age fly all over the place."

Tad sighed. "A jet cycle's AI isn't smart enough to trigger the treaty provisions, Pete, and you're going beyond the one-light-minute treaty limit for back-up telecontrol. It's a technicality, I admit — April could certainly throw switches if something went wrong. But we honor technicalities."

"So I need another qualified pilot?"

A long pause, then, "Pete, Ahmed has gotten a little ahead of the power curve, as far as Spacetrans is concerned. Spacetrans is a Cislunar company, but the board still has an Earth majority. I don't think the P.M. wants to put vacuum in their hoses yet, even with a life at stake."

Our current prime minister was as tough with his own people as he was soft with Earth. That, everyone said, would change with the next election.

"Even Jeanette's?"

Tad shook his head. "Look, she's family, but she's burned family bridges, too, with her thoughtlessness. Do you still care that much?"

I didn't answer. I wasn't sure how well Tad could read my face through a space helmet visor from a wrist comp cam, but I just stared at it. Yes, I did care... no, I didn't. Go figure it out.

Whatever passed on that staring channel passed. Tad cleared his throat. "Listen carefully, Pete. We have to deal with political realities. *Listen carefully.* I think I've given you enough information. More than some people would want me to give out. I've got to call it a conversation, now. Good luck. Reynolds out."

Listen carefully? It just occurred to me that someone else might be listening too.

Honor technicalities? The AI would. Good luck, he'd said. If I were up to grasping at straws, there may be straws to grasp. But if I wanted an excuse to walk away from it, well, I'd been given it. No one, not even Jeanette's family, would blame me. The whole damn thing was back on my shoulders.

"Hmm," Tamika said. "The protocol articles specify human control redundancy. Piloting redundancy is a Cislunar Republic requirement, which can be met by the AI. *They are not the same requirement.* As an adult with a degree in philosophy and a minor in logic, I could more than satisfy the human control redundancy requirement, and you and the *Korolev*'s computer would satisfy the piloting redundancy requirement. You don't have to have two qualified pilots."

Ahmed slapped a hand down on the desk in front of him. "They would call that evading the spirit of the law."

"But not the letter," Tamika said.

"Is it cheating?" April asked. "Ethically?"

Tamika frowned deeply. "No," she said at last. "It is uncomfortably close, but it balances what is uncomfortably close to misuse of law by the other side, I think. And there is the possibility of saving a life to tip the balance toward the greater good."

Left unsaid was the possibility of harm to her; the possibility of losing April, and possibly me — to an accident. Or her losing me to Jeanette if we succeeded. Could my little family be put back together again? Only three or four years ago, I would have asked nothing more of this universe. Could I resist an attempt by Jeanette to do so now, once we were on Mars?

"Ethically," Ahmed said. "I think Allah will forgive us for trying. And I think others will forgive us if we succeed. This is not a business for cowards. Jinn," he addressed his AI, "put another fluid bed on the *Korolev*, and compose a new flight plan with Tamika as cybernetics officer. Our move."

Ahmed had been the Lunar chess champion a few years ago, I recalled. He had moved quickly and the opponent had run out of time in
the end game. But...

"No!" I said. "Ahmed, wait!"

Everyone stared at me.

"Jinn, hold that." Ahmed looked deflated. "But I do not blame you,
friend."

"It's not that," I said. "We need to do what you were going to do.
Kelly and his friends will attack the new flight plan with every argument they can think of. *If* we give them time to do so."

"Of course," Tamika said, "but...?"

"Let's get everything ready, and then file the plan at the absolute
last second. Ahmed, while it's being filed, call Kelly. He's probably got
us flagged, but if he's busy, the human approval will go to a lieuten-
ant. And file a return plan for our hopper at the same time."

A big grin split Ahmed's face. "And a hover test plan for one of my
other spacecraft. While I am discussing his rules with him..." he
laughed. "They will be saturated, and while these discussions go on..."
he raised his flat hand up from the desk toward the ceiling. "...off you
go!"

Half an hour later, off we went. The *Korolev* lifted itself gently on
its auxiliary jets to about ten kilometers altitude and put itself
between the beam projector and Mars. "Fairy dust" rose toward us,
flashed into plasma, and we leapt Marsward. But I hardly noticed the
acceleration because, on the screen above me, Kelly's face turned livid
at the bull Ahmed gave him.

I'll give Kelly credit, it had only taken him fifty seconds to catch
onto what had happened. But in those fifty seconds we had reached
lunar escape velocity.

"Emergency abort!" he thundered. "Override the experimental
field's AI!"

We could hear the port AI respond over our link. "There is no
emergency," it said. "However, interrupting a beam launch in progress would endanger the occupants, creating an emergency. The
abort cannot be executed."

"I'm telling you on human authority that there is an emergency,"
Kelly tried.

Tamika giggled, and in a second I realized why. Kelly was trying to get a state-of-the-art exaflop cybernetic system with full access to all the information into an Asimovian logic loop. It had probably checked every possibility and modeled the psychology of its reply a dozen times before Kelly even finished speaking.

"The telemetry on the spacecraft shows no immediate danger. Could you please specify your reason for thinking there is one? Also, cutting the beam now would leave the spacecraft on a very inconvenient trajectory for rescue. Do you wish to take responsibility for a command override?"

Kelly opened his mouth, then shut it and stared. Finally, he said. "Fahsi, first *you* figure out a way to get them back while I call some *people*. Then, I'd get ready to clean out your desk. Kelly out."

"Having a clean desk is a good idea," Ahmed replied smoothly. "Perhaps at the end of the day will see whose is most clean. Mine, or yours. Fahsi out."

Kelly's face vanished.

Ahmed's replaced it, and he looked worried. The "secure" superscript indication appeared on our screen. He glanced up to where he knew the notation would appear to us.

"They'll know we have a secret now, but I need to tell you this. We dodged one there; the trajectory is not that inconvenient for us to abort, but the port AI did not realize that because there are some things about this that even my AI does not know. But, if they think of it, the Deimos base projector can send a beam to push you back toward the Moon from almost any point between here and there.

"If you want to avoid that, you will have to quench your magnetic field, then bring it up again twenty gigameters out from Deimos. At that point, the only plausible abort will be to Deimos and they will be faced with a fait accompli. But while your field is quenched, you will be vulnerable to solar radiation storms, so let us hope you think of something else."

"*Us* think of something else?"

It was almost a second before Ahmed replied. Half a second of lightspeed delay already!

"They will break into this supposedly secure link in seconds if they have not already done so, but they cannot break into your minds.

Anticipate. Use the lightspeed delay to act instead of react. Now, Allah be with you."

"Ahmed," Tamika said. "You have taken a great risk; rightly, I think. But what are you going to do?"

We waited a second and then saw a smile on Ahmed's face.

"I should not say everything. But for one thing, I will call a press conference. Ahmed out."

Act instead of react.

"Will they push us back with the fairy dust?" April asked.

"It's possible. I depends on who's in charge of what, I guess."

She sighed. "Well, it's too bad about Mom then. But I guess as moms go, she's about a three. I can deal with it."

"April!" They teach kids fuzzy logic in fourth grade now; nothing is either/or anymore — it's all on a scale of one to ten.

"Pete," Tamika said, "she's really just saying what Tad was saying — only being more honest. April, remember your ethics. What's the equivalent inverse situation to your donating a lung to your Mother?"

"Her donating a lung to me? Oh. I see. Do you think she would? Dad?"

What would you do, Jeanette? Would you come back from Mars? You wouldn't come back to raise your kid, but would you come back to save her life? Or would there be an excuse?

"Sure she would, kid." I said. Why make things any worse?

"If we lived," Tamika added, "in the sort of society where you would not make the effort to save her, it would also be a time in which, I think, she would not make such an effort to save you. Good deeds, I think, lend their way to an atmosphere of good deeds, so even if there is no direct reciprocity, all benefit. Meanness, on the other hand, leads to emulation as well. Be careful 'not to do unto others as you would not wish done unto yourself'."

"Jesus?" April asked.

"In a way. But first, K'ung Fu Tze."

April sighed. "I feel heavy."

We were in skin-tight vacuum suits floating in oil, nominally in the zero gravity of neutral buoyancy. Still, there were cues. There was no oil in my helmet and my tongue felt heavy. I could feel the skin on my face sag.

♂ ♂ ♂

Ahmed looked grim. He was transmitting in the clear. "They will make me shut off the beam soon. I am sorry. The beam from Phobos will arrive in two hours to push you back. Ahmed out."

But before his face vanished, he gave us a wink. Obviously, he thought we still had a chance.

"The splash is already getting dimmer," Tamika said.

I looked to my right, at the screen showing the ring center. The "splash" was where the incoming fairy dust blasted itself into plasma and was reflected by the magnetic field. It was dimming — that meant less energy. But I felt just as heavy — we were still doing four gravities. How...? Of course!

"More mass, less velocity," I said finally. "Energy goes with mass times velocity squared, but thrust just scales directly with mass times velocity. Twice as much mass at half the relative velocity gives the same push, but needs only half as much energy. So the splash is dimmer.

"But that's not why he did it. The lower velocity stuff takes longer to get to us, so it has to leave earlier — he's figured out a way to send us all the push we need before they shut him down!"

"Does that mean his beam will still be pushing us when the Phobos beam hits us?" Tamika asked.

"Probably." I tried to imagine us caught between two blobs of plasma, one trying to push us to Mars, the other trying to push us back to the moon.

"Dad," April said. "If we move a little, will our fairy dust follow our ultraviolet beam? Like Mr. Fahsi showed us?"

"Yes. Well, maybe." The sideways thrust of Ahmed's particles had to be minuscule. "*Korolev*, what kind of sideways delta v can the beam follow?"

"About half a millimeter a second at this distance."

"Get started," I said and focused my eyes on Polaris. "That way."

"We are already moving that way at almost a meter per second, to stay in the beam center. The beam is not tracking us exactly, so *we* have to track *it*. This is not normal, but within our limits."

"Of course! Ahmed's giving us some maneuvering room. Okay, you give us half a millimeter a second at right angles to that, just in case the bad guys figure it out."

"Done."

"Can the Phobos mass beam find us," Tamika asked, "if we don't give it a UV beam to follow?"

I had a moment of hope, then remembered one of the redundancies. "Damn. Unfortunately, yes. Ahmed has corner cubes along the ring just in case the ship's UV lasers fail. As a back-up, the beam site can shoot a laser at us, and the incoming particles can follow its reflection as if it was our own laser." But, I thought... "But not if we cover them. *Korolev*, can you cover the retroreflectors?"

"Not at this acceleration. My robot's servo motors can't lift their own arms in this."

"Why didn't Ahmed give them stronger motors!"

The question was rhetorical, but the *Korolev* answered it. "These are lunar robots that were put aboard at the last instant."

Of course. "Can we reduce the reflector field to what they can handle?"

"We can, but then we would not be in position to rendezvous with a deceleration beam at the end of the coast period. Also, I cannot reduce it quickly; the energy tied up in the reflector's magnetic field has to be radiated away and we don't have a full complement of radiators."

"How slow can you go and still make the rendezvous if you give it an hour?"

"Three point one four two gravities."

"Let's try three point two."

"My robots cannot..."

"Not your robots. Me."

I lift weights — most lunar folk do. The image of lunies as weaklings haunts us and some of us overcompensate; lunar weight lifters have won three Olympic weight lifting medals even though the population of the moon is less than that of a large city on Earth. I even lift when I'm on Earth, where I was just a month ago. The human body has a lot of margin built into it; they say we can take four gravities almost indefinitely.

But, truth be told, I hadn't been lifting that much. When the *Korolev* got down to three point two gravities, I damn near couldn't get out of my acceleration tank. I learned very quickly that I had to plan every step. Over to the life support chest with the john in it —

there was a tool kit in there as well. Rest standing — I didn't dare sit down. Over to the door. Rest.

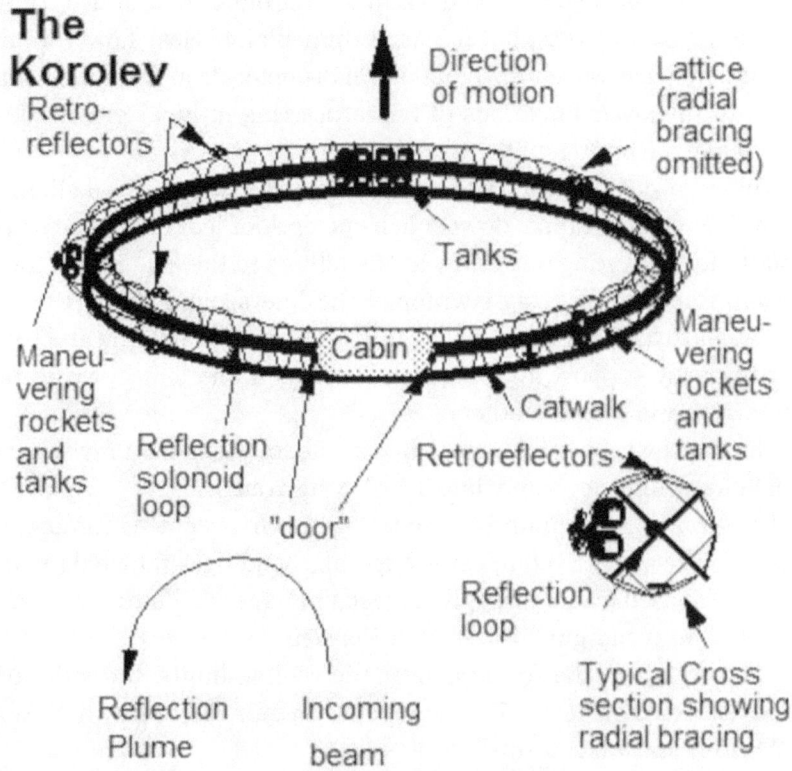

The Korolev

Retro-reflectors

Direction of motion

Lattice (radial bracing omitted)

Tanks

Maneu-vering rockets and tanks

Cabin

Maneu-vering rockets and tanks

Reflection solonoid loop

"door"

Catwalk

Retroreflectors

Reflection loop

Reflection Plume

Incoming beam

Typical Cross section showing radial bracing

When this was all over, my near middle-aged body was going to pay for it, big time. Every ordinary motion seemed to take an extraordinary effort — it was much more tiring, initially, than just the additional weight would suggest. I had to take the "door" panel off myself — we hadn't sealed and pressurized yet, but it still took fifteen minutes to get my head out of the *Korolev*'s cabin.

The "splash" was a huge, brilliant, violet ball below the ring with a spike stabbing up through it as a small portion of the plasma escaped along the magnetic field lines that went through the center of the ring. The black tube of the reflector electromagnet ran overhead through the center of the framework supported by big "X" braces every five meters — a ring within a ring. Actually, with all the force from the plasma being applied to the magnet, the ring frame was hanging from the loop rather than loop supported by the frame.

At my present weight, the lattice structure of the ring looked downright flimsy. There was a catwalk on its bottom, but it definitely did *not* look designed for someone to walk around on it at over three gravities. Not only that, but it wasn't immediately clear how I would get on it — what was an insignificant half-meter drop from the cabin frame to the lower longerons of the lattice ring in lunar gravity now looked like the bottom of the Grand Canyon.

You'd go down a wall like that by rappelling, I realized. It may seem ridiculous to rappel down a half-meter door ledge, but that's just what I did, anchoring one of my safety tethers to the hole in a vertical longeron above the door. I wrapped the line around the shaft of a universal driver from the tool kit as a kind of friction bearing and used that to partly support my weight as I dropped one foot down to the framework and then the other.

Next to the cabin and a cross beam, the longeron held my weight. Still holding onto the safety line, I took a step out.

The frame bent under me, curving down over a centimeter, I guessed. The groan of composite longerons bending conducted its way from the abused frame through my feet and bones and into my ears.

"What's my margin?" I asked the *Korolev*.

"The stress on the frame is over the redline limits, but still 20% below expected strength. I am compensating for the frame distortion with active tension controls."

Okay. I told the clip on the safety line to release itself, reeled it in, and stretched to attach it to one of the magnetic loop supports ahead of me. Supporting part of my weight with the safety line and part with my feet, I took a first tentative step. There were guide wires, but they didn't look like they would support any significant weight; I ignored them and hung on to the safety line.

The catwalk bent alarmingly, but didn't break. I took another step. This got me close enough to reach forward and attach my second safety line to the next support. I had to rest after the simple act of holding my arm above my head long enough attach the clip.

So. Half brachiating on safety lines and half walking, I got to the first retroreflector. It was a full five meters over my head — an insignificant height on the moon, but a mountain in these circumstances.

Plan A had been to climb up there somehow and detach it with my tool. No way.

Plan B was my flare pistol. I took careful aim from almost directly below, bracing my shooting arm on the frame. The minirocket from my first shot missed to the right and I was rewarded by a brilliant flare high above the spacecraft.

The second shot hit the frame below the retroreflectors platform with a shower of sparks — and the smashed minirocket fell at incredible speed, missing me by a few centimeters. The third shot hit the right side of the retroreflectors platform and did nothing obvious. I put my arm down and rested. I could think of nothing to do but try once more.

This time, the platform tilted, breaking free on one side.

Another shot missed. If I could just hit it one more time...

I did and was rewarded by the entire retroreflector falling down through the frame and into the plasma ball below me. It had taken almost 45 minutes. I knew without asking that my act of half swinging on the safety lines was too slow. I would have to risk my entire weight to the flimsy catwalk. I resolved to move swiftly — things take time to yield and break.

Getting started was the hard thing, like diving into a cold lake. I knew it would probably work — 20% margin in theory — just like you know that, in theory, you'll survive that cold plunge into the lake. But I didn't feel that way. That catwalk could snap, dumping me into the white-hot splash ball below me. I stood there, frozen by doubt, and took another look up at our destination, as if that would fix my resolve again.

It did. As I looked, Mars instantly changed from its normal bright red to an incredibly brilliant purplish gray. They had started, damn them, and I still had two retroreflectors to disable. I turned to make my way back to the cabin. Pete, they've beaten you. Face it. You don't care that much. I could take getting beaten, but did I want April to see me give up this way — with her Mom's life at stake? Tamika's words haunted me — suppose things were the other way around? What if it were April's life at stake? Why the hell couldn't those idiots in charge of the mass beams and the lasers see that — it could be them! What business was it of theirs to stop me?

I became very focused. Risk to myself and others, feasibility, the whole ambiguity of my mission faded into the background. I was trying to do something and someone else was trying to stop me. It was now a contest of will and having come this far, I intended to win it or die in the attempt.

My anger gave me the surge of adrenalin I needed, and before I could talk myself out of it again, I turned and almost threw my right leg onto the catwalk.

Down it bent, but I had my left leg ahead before it finished bending. Walking on the catwalk between the X braces was like walking on a rubber sheet, but it didn't break immediately and I didn't stop long enough to find out if it would; it must have taken me less than two minutes to get another third of a circle around the ring to the X-brace of the second retroreflector.

I attached a safety line, sagged against it, and rested.

When I caught my breath, I shot the retroreflector off with five minirockets. Getting better, I thought.

But I was sore, terribly sore. There was a sharp pain in my right knee. There was an incredible tension in my neck, and I couldn't massage it in the vacuum suit. One more retroreflector.

I charged out along the rubbery catwalk faster this time and arrived slower and exhausted. It took me minutes to catch my breath and summon enough energy to raise the pistol.

With my body too tired to shake, my first shot hit right where I wanted it, and the retroreflector's platform tipped and fell back with a crash that set the whole X-brace vibrating. Out of alignment, definitely, but the thing about corner-cube reflectors is that they don't have to be aligned. I had to get it off entirely. One more shot would do it.

I pulled the trigger and nothing. The magazine was supposed to have twenty shots, and I'd only fired twelve. I looked at it; eight shots remaining. Did a minirocket misfire? Was it still sitting in the launch tube? Did I dare look? What would happen if it was and I fired another rocket into its ass?

I was tired, tired, tired. Three point two gravities were killing me.

Three point two gravities? I took the flare gun, pointed the launch tube down and gently tapped it against the X brace. With a sudden clatter, the bad round fell out of the gun and onto the catwalk. It lay there, bright red and just as dangerous as the color suggested.

Brilliant, Pete. Why didn't you, I asked myself, do the tapping with the launch tube pointed down into the splash? Now, do you just leave it there and risk either its propellant charge or its flare going off at some inopportune time, or do you knock it off the catwalk and risk triggering it then and there, with a foot or hand involved?

What was done was done. Recriminations could wait. Which way was the damn thing pointed? Toward the cabin, of course. It would knock a hole through it, fry the inside with its exhaust, and put another hole in the opposite side while it exited.

I took the universal driver, placed its ten-centimeter shaft next to the bad round, and gently pushed the nose of the little rocket so its nose pointed out away from the cabin and its exhaust end pointed in toward the center of the ring. It didn't go off. Maybe I could get rid of it entirely. No, I thought, don't borrow any more trouble. Leave it there.

I turned upward, neck protesting, and looked at the retroreflector's platform. I braced my arm, shot, missed, shot again, and the flare went off when it hit. I shut my eyes *hard*. The inside of my helmet stank, I realized. I didn't want to think of what the rest of my body would smell like when I got out of the tightsuit. I dreamed of a hot tub. If one had been available just then, I might have given up on everything else and jumped in it.

When I opened my eyes, I could see nothing but haze at first. There were lights and displays inside my helmet, but I couldn't see them. I waved my hand in front of my faceplate. Nothing. I blinked hard and opened them again. This time, out of the corner of my left eye, there was something. My air indicators which should be a pair of green, yellow or red circles were a kind of gray and shapeless blob. I blinked again — clearer this time. I let out a long sigh.

"Pete, Tamika." There was a lot of concern in her voice. "Are you all right? It looked like a minor nova out there."

"Tell me about it. My eyes are still recovering — bright spots floating around in front of me. I can't see the retroreflector. Is it still there?" How was I going to shoot it off if I couldn't see clearly?

"It's gone, Pete."

Done it. Somehow I'd gotten it done. The Phobos beam couldn't find us now until we wanted it to. But I needed rest; whatever energy I had left in me evaporated as soon as I knew I'd succeeded. I was

literally sitting in the harness to which my safety line was attached —
the legs were completely gone.

"I'm going to stay out here until acceleration stops; I can't move
another meter."

"No, Pete," Tamika said. "We have to increase acceleration again.
You need to get back to your fluid bed. Another sixty meters. You can
do another sixty meters."

I groaned. "No way."

"Turn up your oxygen."

"Oxygen?"

"That's what those heavy professional athletes do on Earth."

"Okay."

I focused on the left blob and said "up." It blinked, signifying an
increase of five percent. I did that six more times and breathed
deeply. My vision started clearing more rapidly.

"Okay," Tamika asked. "Can you move now?"

I could.

"Come on, then."

Okay, I told myself. If she wants me to do it, I should. I owe her. I
gathered myself for one more mad slow-motion dash for the cabin
that got slower and slower and slower and wobblier and wobblier. My
knee was killing me, and halfway there I had to shut my eyes to
concentrate on moving it, blinking open just often enough to put my
feet on the catwalk. It helped somehow to forget about the goal
however many meters ahead and just concentrate on moving my
exhausted body.

I ran into something, of course. An X-brace. At least it was in a
place where the catwalk didn't sag. Time to rest again, and this time,
oxygen or no, I really had to lie down.

But I opened my eyes first, and found I was almost there. April and
Tamika were there in the cabin "door," arms extended, urging me on.
Just two meters left. Panting, I somehow held myself up, gained a
little strength and hurled myself forward and in three heroic steps,
crashed into the cabin wall. While I rested to gain strength for that
one last climb into the cabin, I took one more look up.

Mars was red again. The Phobos guide laser had been turned off,
or at least was no longer pointed in our direction. Whether it was
Ahmed's random course shifts, our tiny maneuver, or disabling the

retroreflectors, something had worked. We were going to get to Mars. Maybe in time.

♂ ♂ ♂

Whatever memories I had of climbing back into the cabin and into my acceleration bed were gone once I woke up. It was dark, but I could see by the Mars light relayed by our viewscreens. Mars showed a visible disk now — better than half way. Tamika must have sealed and pressurized the cabin — the normally tight parts of my vacuum suit were slack. I confirmed this with a glance at my helmet's heads-up display.

So I was able to take off the helmet for the first time in twelve hours. The cabin was completely silent — whatever fans were at work were too far buried to be heard. When they finish work on the *Korolev* it will rotate for centrifugal gravity, but for us, the coast phase of our journey was in zero gravity. How had I gotten here, I wondered. I remembered Tamika and April beckoning.

"Tamika?"

"Oh, you are awake. Thank goodness! We have about twenty minutes before deceleration. I have set up the shower..."

Even in zero gravity, every muscle in me seemed to scream with pain as I moved.

Ahmed had not stinted on the shower — it cycled a gallon a minute — warm soothing water and hot air flowing over me and sucked into the grate below. If only the twenty minutes had lasted longer...

♂ ♂ ♂

I listened to Ahmed's news conference on the way back in to Phobos. He smiled; he was very polite; he only answered questions and told the truth — but he answered questions in such detail that I was sure Kelly would not be employed on the Moon much longer.

Nor would his immediate superior, who had acted against us without Tad Reynolds' approval and had thereby brought the weight of both official and public wrath upon himself.

I also learned that, so far, our effort was not in vain. Jeanette was still alive.

♂ ♂ ♂

We were met in space off Phobos by an old fashioned reentry shuttle — there was no time to go out to Deimos to take the elevator down to Ascraeus Mons. And no time for the press conference that would have entailed.

The shuttle commander and sole crewmember was a thin young woman with a very prominent nose and a smile to match. She met us at the door, towed us to our seats, and saw that we were strapped in. We hopped over to the Phobos maglev port and in minutes were on a trajectory to the Jovis Tholis dome. As soon as she cut the rockets, she asked for everyone's autograph.

April slept until the landing. But Tamika had something to say.

"Jeanette wants more than a new lung," she said.

So I had to face it. I opened my mouth but nothing would come out.

"Life," Tamika said, "doesn't always let us be happy. If you choose to stay with Jeanette, I will hurt, but I will be able to deal with that. I understand the beauty of restoring something that was once broken, and how that would appeal to you. If you weren't like that, I wouldn't love you so much. So I can't have it both ways, can I?"

We were strapped into seats across an aisle. I couldn't hug her — or be hugged.

"You are a real philosopher, Tamika," I said, and mouthed a kiss at her.

She shook her head and I could see tears in her eyes. "No, not so philosophical now. Now I am just a woman begging for her man. What philosophy that I can give you is that when you cannot be happy yourself, at least do that which creates the least unhappiness for others."

"Tamika, I..."

"No. Tell me after you talk to Jeanette. For you will not have really decided until then."

"However I feel about Jeanette, I still love you."

The roar of our entry into the Martian atmosphere made further conversation impossible.

♂♂♂

Everything is efficient on Mars — we were met by a robot ambulance with its own universal pressure ramp. Dazed, the three of us unstrapped ourselves and followed the shuttle pilot in and were on our way. April was under anesthesia less than two hours after touchdown on the Jovis Tholis university field.

Three hours later, Dr. Lada Baklinova told us that the operation was a success. Jeanette was already breathing on April's lung, a new heart was starting to bud next to the artificial one, and a new lung was growing in the left cavity next to that. Her prospects were excellent. Aside from the injuries, Jeanette was a strong, healthy woman and it turned out that there'd been little deterioration inside. She'd tolerated the stuff they use to help the prostheses very well. She probably would have lasted a week or two. But it was good that we came as quickly as we had, she said.

If we'd gone at one gravity, I thought, someone would have had time to figure out a way to stop us.

A week later, they brought Jeanette out of a "recuperative coma" and she asked for me. So I was alone, face to face, with her for the first time in eight years. Whether it was fluid retention, relaxation, or something they had given her, her face, as much of it as I could see anyway, looked a dozen years younger. She was radiant.

"Pete, I'm terribly sorry," she said before I had a chance to say anything. "My mistake. I just got caught up in things, really lost sight of priorities. I should have a family, I should belong. Pete, this is a great place to be a family... they're already allocating land. If you get in at the beginning, you could get hundreds of square kilometers... We could found a dynasty. The divorce was a mistake... Let's undo it, start over."

I shut my eyes. I could have it. I could recover a quarter century of my life and give it meaning again.

All I had to do was betray the only truly good person I had ever met. I would never be happy with myself if I did that and I would spend the rest of my life wondering "what if" if I didn't.

"I can't promise anything, Jeanette." Coward, I called myself. Make a decision.

No, I realized, it wasn't solely mine to make. "April needs to be part of this, too."

"This is too big, Pete. She's only twelve."

"Thirteen, Jeanette. She turned thirteen the day before yesterday." We'd gotten a ride to Olympus Mons from Jeanette's boss. He had a lot to say about Mars and little to say about Jeanette other than to call her a "brilliant, determined woman."

Jeanette shut her eyes. "Fine. Thirteen. I've been busy."

"I'll call her in."

April came in and looked uncomfortable. "Hi, Mom, I got a monster scar."

Jeanette smiled more brightly than was natural. "I'll bet you do. Thank you, darling. Thank you so much. April, honey... Pete. Isn't this a wonderful new world?"

I nodded. Next to Luna, it was huge and sprawling. Next to the Earth, uncrowded with lots of elbow room.

"There will be rivers here — and forests. We can be among the first homesteaders. Everyone who's on Mars when they decide to open it up can claim a few hectares. They're starting to give it an atmosphere. In a century or so, we'll be able to run, breathe, swim, and play."

"You're planning on living forever?" I asked.

"I don't see why not. The genetic engineers are close. Very close. Pete, you could share it with me. Forget the divorce, we can remarry instantly. Jovis Tholus dome is five kilometers in diameter and only a tenth of it is allocated. You could go to high school here, April. You'd be one of the first graduates. We could be a family again, just like before."

April's eyes got wide, but then she frowned. "That's kinda like putting a broken egg back together, huh? Mom, this one is pretty broken." April looked up at me, eyes glistening, then bit her lip and tried to look very, very adult. "But I'd like to live on Mars. Could Tamika live with us, too?"

Jeanette opened her mouth to say something, shut it again, composed herself, then said. "I was thinking just us. On Mars, you only have one... person. IPA laws — Mars is a joint project. Anyway, I'm not sure Tamika would go along with that. She'll do okay, April. She did before."

"On the Moon, lots of people share. It's no big deal. Why don't you come back and live with us?"

"April, there's this big new wonderful world. Besides, that..." Jeanette obviously struggled for words, "...wouldn't be fair to Tamika."

"Huh? She's okay. Look, do you want to be part of a family again or what?"

"April!" Jeanette sounded stern. That was a lot of pressure to put on the kid. I wanted to say something sharp, but suppressed it.

April suddenly got a frightened look on her face and threw her arms around me. "Daddy, why does it have to be so hard?"

Why indeed? Leave it to April to suggest a way to have my cake and eat it too. When you're that young, anything seems possible. By middle age, there's just too much social baggage. "I think you were right about the broken eggs, darling. But Jeanette will always be your mother. And there will be plenty of time to be together in years to come. Especially if she's right about living forever."

I smiled and took April's hand and put in Jeanette's. In a minute they were both in tears and April — very carefully — buried her face in her Mother's shoulder. Jeanette closed her eyes for a moment. When she opened them, glistening, I knew she'd given up.

"I'm very sorry, April," she said. "Once in the while the universe lets you put a broken egg back together. We got one put back together — me..." She looked up into April's eyes for a moment, then down. "...so I guess we should be happy with that." She turned her face up to me. "I'm sorry, Pete, I love you both as much as I can love anyone and always will. And I'm very grateful." She sighed and pursed her lips. "But I have to be true to myself. I have to be out here, exploring — that's always going to come first for me. I'd love to have you to come home to, but...but let's keep in touch, birthdays and things, good memories, okay? No hard feelings?" She squeezed my hand and April's.

Dr. Lada Baklinova came into the room then.

"Time to let her sleep, now."

I nodded. It was also decision time. The Martian authorities had taken one look at the *Korolev* and said, privately, that they couldn't in good conscience let anyone go off in space in that unless it was an emergency. Strange things happen, true — but they were betting that it would be several decades before anyone got to Mars from Luna in one day again.

The *CLS Von Braun* was due out today, but they were holding her in case we decided not to stay — the celebrity treatment was Tad Reynolds' doing. He was trying to make amends. But the next ship out wouldn't leave for three months, and that was a four-month voyage with a Venus flyby. The *Von Braun* could get us back in ten weeks.

"Jeanette. They've got a ship waiting for us. We've got to go home now."

There, I said it. I had what I'd dreamed of for all those years offered to me, and I turned it down. Except that it really wasn't my dream. Five. Thirteen. However long we all lived, I'd never get those years back.

She nodded, but looked into my eyes and pleaded with them one last time.

I knelt by her bedside, reached gently across her, and we kissed one last time, for the memories, and all the hurt came back, but it would have been wrong not to do it.

April kissed her mother goodbye, too. For the last time as a child, I thought. Five. Thirteen. Probably twenty-one by the next time they met.

There were no more words and we left, somehow stumbling down the corridors to the reception area. Tamika met us there and herded us, dazed, through the vans, the suborbital shuttles, and up the high speed elevator to Deimos for the ten-week trip back to Luna.

As we approached the *CLS Von Braun,* the sun sparkled off the huge butterfly wings of her radiators and lattice work of her ion accelerators. They reminded me of the sails and halyards of yet another bygone era.

What do we gain?

April hugged me. "She's really more like a six or seven, Dad. Too bad."

Tamika laughed and pointed at herself. April instantly held up ten fingers.

I looked down on the rusty cloud streaked globe of Mars where my first love would make her life.

What do we give up?

AFTERWORD — A LIFE ON MARS

IF WE ARE SERIOUS about going to the stars, as we one day will be, we shall need to create propulsion systems for the job that will, incidental to their main purpose, reduce the temporal size of the solar system to about that of the world in the age of steam. Some twenty-second century writer might then emulate Jules Verne with "A Tour of the Planets in Eighty Days."

Well, to move that fast, don't carry your fuel and engines with you; their mass holds you back. But this requires a transportation infra-structure as constraining and vulnerable as steel rails, highways or air traffic control — with an authority structure to match. So, ultimately the independent, roving spaceship of romantic science fiction will go the way of the lone rider, the stage coach and the pony express of the American (or Australian, or Argentine) frontier.

Technology advancement may kill the rocket era before it is even born, but perhaps there will be a few years of rockets to Luna or Mars, especially if some political earthquake allows the use of nuclear energy for space-to-space rocketry. Rocket voyages in the early days of space exploration will take months, because fuel efficient trajecto-ries are so time consuming. Even so, manned spacecraft will never use the most efficient trajectories, called "Hohmann transfer orbits," because at maximum trip time, trading a day's worth of consumables for same weight of rocket fuel will save several days of travel time. Still, for months at a time the commander of a rocket spacecraft would be a king-like figure and his officers, his nobles. When non-rocket propulsion systems reduce their lord captainships to something more like the more temporary and constrained responsibilities of train conductors, some resistance might be expected.

The isolation of Mars in the early days will, no doubt, figure in many poignant stories of family separation and or choices made between a chance for glory and family. And in that isolation, the kind of character that flourished in the Earthly frontiers, the John Fremonts and the Annie Oakleys, may once again step briefly on the stage of history.

A WORLD TO REMEMBER

A SOFT WHIR caught their attention. A robot? To interrupt a Hive-Father's conversation was not incalculable, but it would have to be something very, very important.

"Honored Hive-Father, Honored Eldest Daughter, something has been found. The original is far too fragile — so it is still mostly encased in rock — but we were able to scan it and make a replica."

It handed the rectangular object to Eldest Daughter, who handed it to Althor.

"It" was a stack of hundreds of thin sheets, bound at the edge so any pair could be viewed without blowing away or getting out of order. After ten revolutions of an occasional decorative pin, this was a find indeed. He opened it at random and scanned the strange characters. He emitted multiple tones and closed it gently, reverently.

"Well! We'd best get going on deciphering this!"

Eldest Daughter took the object and opened it as well, then began turning the sheets.

Suddenly she stopped, tentacles trembling.

"Look. A picture. A planetary system."

"Not this one, it appears. It shows thirteeen major worlds; this system has nine."

"The innermost ones would have been consumed in the red giant stage.

"Four worlds?"

"No, no. Only three. See, they count the ice ball as a world."

"Hmm... if this is to scale, it was a rather large one. With a big moon. If it's gone now, that would leave the inner three to be consumed, then comes what you take to be this world, then the big giant, and the world with the almost homelike moon, and... well, it does fit. The very innermost world, you think?" Althor put a tentacle tip on it. "About the right size."

"Too hot, if the orbits are to scale. This was a big bright star, at least thirty times as bright as our home star. That's why it's gone beyond the red giant phase already." Eldest Daughter put a tentacle tip on the third world. "The temperature would have been right there. The bones tell the rest. Their males were nearly equal in numbers to the females — and while both genders were powerful by our standards, the males were usually bigger, and were born male."

"Hmmm. Then growing up female would have been a different proposition, I suspect. A little more spear-driven than our uppity version!" Althor used upper middle tones of humor for that "Anyway if those two worlds are to scale — why they are huge. One would weigh a gedong there! How could they ever get something off so massive an object, let alone with enough left over to visit other worlds?"

"Hive-Father, it must have been quite a project..."

MARTIAN VALKYRIE

I, ENRICO LOPEZ, am the first man to set foot on Mars and come back alive. But there are moments when I feel a heroic death, like that of Robert Falcon Scott, would have suited me far better. Better than what I must live with, and what I must live without.

Back in Bergen, old man Halvorsen must still be laughing. Yes, he is still alive and intends to live forever. Any day now, the genetic engineers have been saying. Good for him. He does not dare die, I think, for where he is going, they will not be so gentle.

Let him laugh, part of me says. Despite our problems, we got much more scientific data, core samples, measurements, and everything. Our rovers roved, our balloons floated, and our scientists have enough data for a million graduate theses. So, in the long view of things, I suppose it matters not one bit who was first on Mars or how we got back.

Except to me, and to history.

♂ ♂ ♂

Four days out from Earth on our very carefully planned trajectory, things had settled into a nominal routine. The United Nations' official expedition was a four ship orbital armada, with forty carefully chosen and politically representative scientists and astronauts and the latest hardware, including nuclear thermal rockets and power-assisted hard suits. With a trillion dollars spent in planning, programming, research and development before the first cargo ships left low Earth orbit, we had all the requirements covered. As its commander, I would be on the first shuttle down and first on the surface. I had my speech memorized.

I remember the moment everything changed with vivid clarity. I was in my double-sized cabin on our flagship, the *Chang-Diaz,* and had just strapped myself into my bunk and ordered the lights down. I had just started to dream about my wife, Linda, and other women I have known, when two loud tones signaled an event important enough to perturb my sleep schedule. I mention it because, even at the expense of my dignity, I cannot resist this irony. For those who believe in signs, there it is.

A voice followed the chimes. "Enrico, this is Mustaffa." Ahmed Mustaffa was the spacecraft's master and my second for the expedition.

"I am awake. What is it?"

"We just downloaded a message from Thor Halvorsen. That Norwegian lunar expedition — it's departed and it doesn't look like it's going to the moon."

"Where else would it go?" I asked. The Norwegians' tiny, stubbornly independent space exploration effort had just assembled two lunar spacecraft in low orbit. Had they had another accident? Two years ago, they had lost the supplies for a Norwegian lunar base camp when their cargo ships had failed to do the lunar orbit insertion burn. Cut rate space programs are the most expensive kind, I told myself. Would we have to rescue them and sacrifice some or all of our own mission? "What is the message, Mustaffa?"

"All the message said was, 'Norway mission headed toward Mars — Halvorsen.' But there's a press release appended. The file's under 'Halvorsen'."

I suddenly felt cold. It was no accident. Had it been anyone else, I would have taken this as an historical joke, but, a generation ago, Halvorsen had found the buried glacier in the rim of Amundsen Crater near the lunar south pole — with a tenth the usual budget. He took his nation's history of exploration very seriously, and he had all the daring and competence of his forbearers.

My cabin featured a small desk next to my bunk, and over the desk was my vid, a mosaic of sixteen flat high-resolution panels joined seamlessly in a commander-sized interface display. A perk of office, but I had to get out of bed to look at it. I resealed and adjusted my tight suit, undid the velcro restraints, and swung myself out of the bunk so I floated in front of it. The sterile circulating air chilled me — our vents did their job so efficiently that they took even the smell of my body away before it could reach my nose.

"Display the Halvorsen file," I said. Text and a diagram filled the vid.

I stared at the report in disbelief. They had launched themselves on a eighty-eight day trajectory with a chemical rocket, obviously intending to use the Martian atmosphere in an aerocapture maneuver. Many studies going back to the 1980s showed that was a terrible idea. It was too hard, they said, to design a big interplanetary spaceship that would fit behind an aeroshield. They said the density of the Martian atmosphere was too variable to plan a precise thirteen-kilometer-per second aerobraking maneuver. Without it, they said the mission called for some thirty kilometers per second of total delta-V, and this required development of the nuclear-thermal rockets.

Halvorsen had laughed at them then, and now, apparently, had launched his own expedition.

"Mustaffa, one of three things will happen:

"First, and most likely, the Norwegians will kill themselves. They will either burn up or fail to be captured." Perhaps, for a fleeting moment, before good Christian conscience took charge of my thoughts, I even hoped that they would.

"Two," I continued, "if they, by main luck, manage to reach Martian orbit, we will probably have to rescue them. There is no way a ship that small could carry enough fuel for a landing and return, even using aerobraking. They are counting on our supplies and our good hearts to steal a share of our glory." *We* would, of course, perform the rescue. Ungraciously.

"But, if all the above is somehow wrong, the third possibility is that Halvorsen will make us look like idiots." Perhaps I feared that the most. He had been on the original planning committee, but as the expedition had gotten bigger, more complex, more expensive, more politically influenced by the member nations, and more compromised, he'd become more and more obstinate. As one of those experts, I'd had words with him. Finally, he had stormed out of a meeting and not returned.

Now he was saying, in effect, that he'd been right all along and that we'd spent a trillion dollars that could have been spent better elsewhere. I shuddered. If true, the media would dance on the graves of our reputations for years to come. That was the worst case I could imagine.

Imagination, however, was never one of my strong points.

"It will be as Allah wills," Mustaffa said. "But I, for one, will try to avoid doing idiotic things."

"*Sí. Chang-D*, put a telescope on the moon." We were already three million kilometers from Luna, but in a second, Mare Orientale filled the screen — three half rings bisected by the shadow line. It would be full moon back home.

"Center it left of the Farside limb, and give me maximum magnification." Once the sunlit side of the moon was off screen, the video intensity readjusted, and I could almost see the shadowed lunar limb in silhouette against the star clouds of Sagittarius. Tiny specks of light flecked the Farside of Luna now, explorers and settlements now almost a decade old. There was nothing moving, and for a moment I had hope that Halvorsen's announcement was a joke — Halvorsen paraphrasing what Amundsen sent to Scott a century and a quarter ago.

Then I saw them emerge from our moon's shadow. Two spots of light, brighter than any nearby stars. They seemed to be moving slowly relative to each other as well as against the background.

♂ ♂ ♂

A line flashed between the spots of light. What? Of course. It was the specular glint as a cable caught the sun just right. Halvorsen, of course, would have used tethers for artificial gravity, after all our committees and systems analysts had decided they were more problems than they were worth.

"Put a dish on them and listen. Contact Mission Control. I'll be up to ops in a minute."

I slipped into my coveralls. We should have been informed. I would talk to Dr. Worthing, man to man, from the dignity of my command deck at the front of our ship.

But only three or four seconds had passed before: "Mission control wants to talk to you."

Of course. I shook my head hard to stimulate myself, pushed the door at the end of my cabin open and emerged from my cell at the aft end of the octagonal common room like a new bee into a hive. My hatch thunked shut and "Blue shift" crew members glanced at me from each of the four "floors" spaced at equal intervals around the hull. I tried to appear unhurried, and nodded to each of them.

There was a pole down the center of this to guide passers-by, but, in a display of the zero-gravity competence expected of a commander, I jumped for the ops hatch directly from my cabin door.

Command ops occupied the forward end of the cylinder, some nine meters away, and I prided myself on my ability to jump the distance without using the pole, shoot through the opening without touching its sides, and catch myself with my toes.

My little maneuver went unwatched above. Mustaffa was alone, twirling his moustache, his dark eyes intent on the command video display as Dr. Worthing of the U.N. International Space Authority gave their version of events. They, he said, "welcomed all space exploration efforts" but "was concerned about the possible complications of another mission, and in particular, one formulated with so many differences in basic philosophy." This went on for a few minutes, then the ISA signed off.

"Nobody on the back line for me?"

Mustaffa turned toward me and shrugged. "What bureaucrat has the patience for a time lag between speeches? We have half a megabyte download of instructions on how to handle press questions from the ISA. It's GMT midnight at Earthport — the public relations people are asleep."

"The press! Public Relations! *Caramba!* What do we do about Halvorsen's mission?"

Mustaffa shrugged. "It appears we are to continue for now as if nothing has happened."

"But what if they — Get a ground line. I'll talk to Halvorsen myself!"

"Enrico, it is after midnight in Norway and he must be eighty—"

"Wake the old fart up!" I pursed my lips. Halvorsen, for all his obstreperousness, was a legend of space exploration. It wouldn't do to display my anger to the crew. "I'll take it in my cabin."

I'd worked for the U.S. NASA for twenty-three years, but I was dark-complexioned, had straight black hair, and had retained my Argentine citizenship. This had made me politically acceptable as the U.N. expedition commander — and a target for some of Halvorsen's criticism. So, if he succeeded in beating us to Mars, he would get back at me, and prove me not only wrong, but unnecessary.

It took twenty minutes, but Mars Mission Control made the connection and I saw the old, straight-backed, craggy-faced, iron-haired descendent of Viking barbarians, dressed in a night robe, frowning at me in what seemed to be a living room. At least the backdrop was a great stone hearth strewn with models of rockets and moon rocks.

I started by asserting my authority as leader of Earth's official expedition and taking an attitude of outrage. "What do you think you are doing? Over."

Forty seconds of lightspeed delay gives one time to question one's wording with no opportunity for recall. I was talking to a man many years my senior and an acknowledged legend. This was not a pleasant way to converse.

"Well," he said, pronouncing his "W" as if it were a "V." "I am sitting in my home listening to Grieg. Per and Ingrid are going to Mars. Over."

The same crew that had gone to the moon with him. Per Nordli was a cool, tall, diffident brown-haired man. He had no cojones, but was otherwise respectable. But his wife looked and acted like someone more comfortable in a bikini than a spacesuit. Make that half a bikini.

"You sent that bimbo Karinsdatter!" I shut my eyes to regain my composure. I needed to interface with his technical staff on flight plans, to prepare contingencies, before we got too far away for comfortable discussion. "Where are your people, your mission control center? I was told you are heading a mission control operation. Over."

While I waited for his response, I shuddered to think of the problem Karinsdatter represented. Our Mars expedition was full of men from developing Islamic, Oriental, and Hispanic cultures — and the sponsoring nations thought the first mission would be hard enough without sexual complications. We had carefully negotiated a decision not to include women on the first mission. Now Halvorsen, on his own, had decided otherwise. Bad enough — but for him to send Dr. Ingrid Bodil Karinsdatter, however theoretically qualified, to Mars was an unforgivable insult.

Yes, for some it would be insulting just because she was a woman. But the problem was more because of the *kind* of woman she was. After she had become famous, she spoke up for population control efforts in opposition to many of the religious leaders of Earth. She used a non-traditional feminist surname. She had posed for that magazine. I and other NASA astronauts — especially the women — had publicly blasted her for that. In return, she made comments about American prudery. But, I am told, the reaction was little different in Norway.

Was Ingrid Karinsdatter someone to dangle before forty men fifty million miles from Earth? Ten of my crew were from conservative Islamic countries. Now, in the Norwegians, I faced a culture whose ideals of womanhood were ski champions, marathon runners, Valkyrie warriors, prime ministers, or Viking queens with names like Aud the Deep Thinker. To that, add the crazy license with which all these modern European women display themselves now that the fear of AIDS has gone.

I stared, tight-lipped, at the large, but simple and spare living room behind Halvorsen, waiting for transmissions to go there and back. Finally he shrugged, almost as a Frenchman would.

"I recruited Per and Ingrid who were with me on the Amundsen Crater expedition. Their children are old enough to leave alone now and I am too old and too blind to do anything but think and talk. But I still do that not too bad, *nei*? *Ja*, I know how you talk of Ingrid." He laughed. "You are not alone, but that is your problem. She knows space. As for mission control, this is it such as it is. I use my house computer and my videophone."

So their standing army was this old half-blind man standing in front of me. Who did he think he was? Goddard? Korolev? Von Braun?

"Oslo University," he continued, "is giving me time on their radio telescope and some volunteer help. That is all. We only have a two person expedition, assembled from standard modules. Over."

I frowned. The Norwegians had bought their way into space with oil money and a cut-rate single-stage shuttle design that NASA had smothered to death. It had a payload of five tonnes to a five-hundred kilometer orbit at best. And they'd hardly changed a thing since their moon escapade. There was no way they could reasonably hope to get a round trip out of that, I thought. They were planning on using *us* — they had to be — and that made me angry.

"This isn't fair, Halvorsen. Our lives may be put at risk. Now will you tell Per Nordli to follow our lead; to do just what we say? So we can get him and his wife back safely? Over."

I waited. Halvorsen's expression changed to ice when he got my transmission. "*Nei*! We plan that they get back by themselves! As for putting lives at risk, you do things so stupid and complex it is *you* that may all die. That is why I walked out of your meetings. *Uff Da!* Bureaucrats, empire builders, and egomaniacs. Bah!" Across six million kilometers and through two sets of communications electronics, this craggy gray old Viking speared me with the contempt in his nearly sightless eyes. "It is too late to be talking such nonsense. Halvorsen out!"

The image dissolved to a UN link operator who told me that Halvorsen had hung up, not waiting for my sign-off. In retrospect, I may have been too peremptory myself, but still, the insult stung.

I called a staff meeting to decide how to deal with the Norwegian expedition. It would take us four days to rendezvous with our Deimos supply depot, refuel, deploy our landers, and be ready to mount any kind of an operation, we reasoned. The Norwegians would most likely have trouble during aerobraking, so it would be best if we were in place before they got there.

Nobody wanted to call it a race, but we examined at our trajectory margins to see if we could get to Mars earlier. The trajectory people told us the time to have done *that* was in low Earth orbit. Now, it would eat into our reaction mass budget more than mission rules would allow. The Norwegians, it seemed, would get to Mars orbit before us. Dead or alive, but first.

Not if I had my way. We had plenty of fuel margin — there ought to be some way of stealing a little of that to shave some days off our trajectory. There was a planned mid-course burn only forty hours away. If it was just a little bigger... I knew my way around mission planning bureaucracies — I called the man in charge of trajectory analysis and asked him if he could run some contingency cases that had looked good to us. Strictly hypothetical? I grinned at the planner and he grinned back. He wanted to win, too.

It looked good.

♂ ♂ ♂

Two days later, I was smiling and it was Halvorsen who was angry.

"We plan so our ships will be out of your way. Now we all get there at once bam-bam and will all be so busy that no one will have time to help anyone! And you use up your fuel margin! Over!"

"You are mistaken in your exaggerations, Dr. Halvorsen," I answered, calmly. Dr. Obote, our ground orbit analyst, also exaggerated when he'd called to upbraid me for my non-nominal burn. But after a few Swahili expletives, he acquiesced to the *fait accompli* and participated in the "discretionary-modification-well-within-mission-parameters" official cover.

"My fuel margin," I continued to Halvorsen, "is *not* used up and we will arrive in Mars orbit well ahead of you. For which you should be profoundly thankful if we have to rescue your people. Now that possibility is an *unplanned* complexity and need for coordination. Over."

I relaxed and contemplated our trajectory display with a smile. The arrival time difference was up to five hours, now — in our favor.

Finally, Halvorsen frowned and opened his mouth. "We have sufficient redundancies and do not require or plan on your help. You have enough problems just executing all you have planned. I ask you now to forget we are there and concentrate on *your* task. Over."

I prayed for equanimity in the face of such arrogance, and my prayer was answered — with the Lord's help, I did not lose my temper, but instead answered in measured tones. "I'm very sorry you feel that way. But we can't let past disagreements stand in the way. When we... I mean, *if* it may be necessary for me to rescue your people, I will need your cooperation. Over."

I waited a minute to hear him snort and shout, "Halvorsen out!" Touchy *hombre*, Halvorsen.

♂ ♂ ♂

We watched the Norwegians on our telescopes as it approached time for their course correction. Our ships were getting closer every day, on paths that would arrive at Mars separated only by hours, and within the last week had gotten close enough so our twenty-meter baseline synthetic aperture optics could see the details of their ship's construction.

Each Norwegian ship appeared to be a bundle of four squat cylinders sitting on their ends in a saucer-shaped heat shield. Range and apparent angle told me the cylinders were each about four meters tall and two meters wide. The cylinders were capped by transparent domes, through which we could occasionally make out one or both of the crew members. There were four holes in the heat shield, one under each cylinder, apparently for the rocket exhaust.

The ships were tied nose-to-nose by a tether almost half a kilometer long, rotating every fifty seconds; at high magnification, it was like watching the second hand of a clock move. We expected to see that clock stop and watch the Norwegians dock, untether, undock, do their burns, rendezvous, redock, re-tether and, in what should be one of the dicier maneuvers in astronautics, reestablish their tethered rotation. I looked at the clock — they were seriously behind schedule if they were going to meet their window. Had something gone wrong already?

Suddenly, one of the ships spouted fire for a couple of seconds. The acceleration was apparently much less than their centrifugal weight, because there was no sign of slack or vibration in the cable.

Twenty five seconds later the other ship also fired when its engines were pointed in the same direction as those of the first ship when it had fired. This went on for five cycles. Nothing wobbled, nothing broke. Mustaffa, as dumbfounded as I was, looked from the bridge video to me, and back again.

I shook my head. I had no idea of how complex their internal procedures and checks were, but the operation viewed from outside was simple to the point of elegance — yet our engineers had justified management's position of not trying spin gravity by citing the complexity and uncertainty of doing such maneuvers. It was something that had never been done before with a manned spacecraft.

Well, now it had — and that tight spot in my stomach that had materialized as soon as I heard of Halvorsen's mission grew a little tighter. We were up against someone who did not live by the rules of managers, politicians, and tame engineers. He did not respect the *zonas intangibles*. He and his people could do things we could not. It wasn't fair. I thought about Ingrid Karinsdatter. It was most definitely not fair.

♂ ♂ ♂

Midway to Mars, I was forced to have a disciplinary hearing. Planetologist Kadir Ibn Muhunnad caught Sajag Kedar, our biotechnician, examining the Norwegian ships at maximum magnification, something that would have attracted no adverse notice except for the data he saved.

I must explain. The Norwegian ships were still somewhat sunward of us and sun was in near the plane of rotation of the tethered ships, plunging their domes into shadow for about ten seconds each revolution. During this time, glare vanished and one could see inside. The Norwegians seemed to use the dome for relaxation — as a sun deck mostly — there were plants and acceleration couches, but almost no visible equipment.

Whether Dr. Karinsdatter was aware of our surveillance, or whether she would have dressed more modestly even if she had been aware of it, is a matter of conjecture. Our telescopes were larger than the Norwegians carried and I doubted that either of them had thought that we could observe them; we must have been just four very bright stars from their point of view. But Halvorsen, who sent them to plague us? He might have thought of it. Oh, he might have.

In one of Sajag's five-second clips, Dr. Karinsdatter, alone on her couch, chanced to look through her bubble, across the megameter of space between us, through the optics and the electronics, from the view plate, and right into my eyes. It was obvious from what she was doing that she had no idea that anyone was looking back at her at such high resolution. Still, I felt taunted — and much more.

"In my country, she could be shot for this," Kadir told me — as he viewed the video evidence just as compulsively as everyone else. "It is her responsibility not to be seen in such a way."

Sajag was removed from the telescope schedule, but I am sure he was just the one who was careless enough to be caught. We all had access, and we all had times when we were the only ones awake on the ship. Several of us had valid reasons to be studying the Norwegian ships. We edited the logs after the hearing; common sense decrees that not everything be saved for posterity. Not only that, but we did not want to give Halvorsen the satisfaction of knowing what he'd done to us.

The Norwegians gradually passed below us and drew away. Their midcourse maneuver had put them slightly ahead for now, and my hopes for getting permission for an autonomous catch-up burn were about nil. But I was sure I could slip a few more meters per second into the next scheduled one.

♂ ♂ ♂

Another month had passed. Mars became a small, reddish, moon to our eyes, and in our telescope, we seemed to fly over its surface. The communications time lag was approaching six and a half minutes. Soon Earth would pass sunward of us as we coasted uphill to our destination.

We watched each other, we and the Norwegians. Officially, we pretended they did not exist. Unofficially, forty men envied Per Nordli more and more, and praised our Mission plan less and less. We had a few heated arguments, and a broken nose in the *Leonov*.

The Norwegians made no attempt to talk to us either. But time had not solved anything, and I had put off making my contingency plans too long. Our final midcourse maneuver was scheduled in two days and things would be too busy then, and too locked in concrete, to coordinate any trajectory changes with the Norwegians. I called Halvorsen.

With almost six minutes between sender and receiver, one doesn't wait for greetings before proceeding to business. After my testy preliminaries, I asked, "Can you at least tell me what kind of parking orbit they are going to try to achieve? We may be able to match inclinations. Over."

Hopefully time and a little conciliation would put the conversation on a professional basis. We needed to make plans and the communications round trip was eating up time.

His eyebrows went up and a hint of a smile crossed his face. "Commander Lopez, I provided all of this data to Dr. Worthing and your mission control two months ago. Per and Ingrid are not going into a parking orbit. They plan to proceed directly to the surface. Parking orbit is a back-up. Over."

"What?" With Halvorsen, I should not have made assumptions. He stared out of the screen at me as, somewhere deep inside me, a sense of doom started to form. I was dealing with a different kind of human being, a leader who dealt with the laws of nature directly, instead of through intermediaries. Everyone's mission plans went to parking orbit — everyone's except Halvorsen's.

History assaulted my mind when I saw his craggy, ancient face. Some recent — Halvorsen's own incredible Lunar South Pole mission twenty years ago. But in the mists there were Amundsen, Nansen, and, of course, Leif Erikson. As to why Dr. Worthing had not told us? He presumably feared what I might do to make up the time. He feared right.

"Did you receive?" Halvorsen asked. "You are silent too long."

I had forgotten to say "over" and wasted six minutes. I shrugged my shoulders, and struggled for internal peace. I was not an inexperienced astronaut; I led explorations of several major lunar features and was second in command on the mission to the asteroid Eros, the trial for this mission. I'd had all the resources of the United Nations behind me. There was no reason for me to be flustered. But I sat there in front of the screen pickup openmouthed.

"Well," he continued, "The whole thing I will run through while you figure out what you say. *Ja*, ten years ago I left the ISA Mars conference. We have already discussed why. Then I talked to our prime minister who nodded his head to some things and shook it to others. Our space program is a matter of national pride, *ja*, but it has to be a not-so-expensive program.

"So, officially, I had the go-ahead to do a small moon base. The Italians have one, the Tysker, the Nederlanders, even the Svensker!" Halvorsen scowled at this, and it was my turn to smile. If you look at the Scandinavian peninsula, you see not golden fields of Nordic brotherhood, but a line of tall mountains down its middle.

"So our little single-stage-to-orbit *Norgedraken* flew ten missions and twice docked four payloads to big composite disks. Then we sent them both toward the moon. You remember?"

Very well, I remembered. It had been a fiasco. *Both* their seven-million-kroner base modules failed to make nominal Lunar Orbit Insertion burns and had whipped by the moon out into interplanetary space. It had been such a loss to the minuscule Norwegian space program that observers thought that it would pretty much end the thing. But their parliamentary committee had met in closed session and voted more of their oil money for a second attempt.

The old man's face broke into the grin I would expect to see on the face of Satan himself when he acquires Halvorsen's soul. "Well, our real plan that was not. *Nei*, nor did anyone notice where the so-called moon base modules went after they picked up a couple of kilometers per second rounding the moon." Halvorsen raised his eyebrows and I got a sinking feeling as I remembered that the date of the Norwegian Moon base "failure" was within a month of our own Mars supply staging mission.

Halvorsen continued. "Everyone said Halvorsen screwed up. *Ikke sandt*? Not so? Well, we let them think that. Now I will put on the animation of our mission." Halvorsen's face was replaced by a cartoon of the "moon" mission as he narrated. "The big disk was not just a docking structure, it was an aerobraking heat shield, which is how one should go to Mars. I say this to you ten years ago, but all your big rocket companies and everyone who wants to work for one someday say, 'no, no, too risky.' So you then buy lots of big rockets, *Ja*? Well, —"

As the trajectory lines on the animation bent past Luna toward Mars, I forgot myself. I yelled at him despite the fact he hadn't finished talking. "Halvorsen, damn you, we only bought *five* ARIES heavy-lift launch vehicles!" He wouldn't hear that until I was well into regretting I said it, of course.

"...our ships have a mass ratio of seven and an exhaust velocity of three kilometers per second. That gets us to Mars fast, easy. We do some phasing pair burns to make sure we hit things right. Then we go right into the Martian atmosphere like the American Apollo returned to Earth, except we use negative lift to hold us down if there is not so much atmosphere where we come by. So, if air is thin, we skim the mountain tops and get at least capture, then hit our target on second pass, but if average, or more dense, we can land first pass. No matter. After we reach terminal velocity, we use rockets for the last half kilometer per second. The computers they need for this simple stuff weigh only a hundred grams now, so we take five each.

"The supply ships were the trial run for the crew ship. They left two tiny satellites in egg shaped half-Mars-day orbit with their high points at that latitude, good for communications relay and reconnaissance. Then they left four full fuel tanks in low orbit and landed on Mars to make more fuel for our return from carbon dioxide with their solar cells. This is not very efficient, but, with two years to do it, the ground base tanks are now full. This is simple, *Ja*? Now Ingrid and Per will go to the bottom of Chryse, as you do, *ikke sandt*? But they will go straight down. Now — "

My outburst about the heavy lift vehicles arrived then; I could hear my voice in the background. He frowned, then grinned. "*Ja*, Well those big companies with the jobs, what did they build next?" He shook his head in exaggerated sympathy. "Back to Ingrid and Per. They can get themselves there and back with plenty of redundancies and no need for you to be concerned. Our ships we can park in Earth orbit and use again in two years. It is your super-complicated one-time mission about which you need be concerned. Over."

There was too much for me to digest, and no point in discussing things until I had.

"I copy. Thank you for the information, Mr. Halvorsen. Over and out."

I signed off with mixed feelings. My Padre taught me to "not tempt the Lord by putting yourself where only He can rescue you." Good advice in the cold scrublands of Patagonia, and good advice here.

Despite Halvorsen's contempt for conventional political and moral authority, the concepts of forethought, at least, were not foreign to him. "Plenty of redundancies," he'd said. I would hope.

In concept it *was* simple. Elegant. The ISA called it MSR, for Mars Surface Rendezvous, and dismissed it as too risky. At first, my mind boggled at a Mars surface refueling operation. But with everything tied down by Martian gravity, I realized it might actually be less tricky than a tank-module swap on Deimos.

As I reviewed Halvorsen's video, I realized the large spider legs on their supply modules placed the tanks higher than on the *Amundsen* and *Fram,* allowing a passive gravity feed. The compactness of their deceptively simple design impressed me — the same piece of mass often performed two or three functions.

Their base was not too far from where we planned to land, so a rescue contingency would not perturb our mission plan very much. There were only two of them, and they already had their own supplies down. In fact, and this was the first time I remembered thinking in these terms, while their expedition was minuscule compared to ours, they had a *lot* of stuff for only two people.

Halvorsen's sign-off arrived as I was thinking it through. "Commander. What is now done is done. Mars will be a hard enough opponent, without false pride to fight as well. I tell this to Ingrid too. You should know she is in charge overall. She is the older, and has the broader education, and is a better English talker. Per is the best pilot and likes to do orbits and numbers mostly, though he can do the other too in a pinch. No matter. They do the job. If you meet my people, you will find Ingrid not so hard to work with."

I stared at the screen speechless, not believing what I'd heard. Halvorsen's commitment to women's equality was well known, and it was one of the many issues over which he had pulled out of the U.N. project. He felt an all-male expedition, especially a large and long one, could become too restive, too grumbly, too combative. But third world politics had gone against him, and he had stomped out. Now he was having his revenge by decreeing that I would have to treat this woman, whose mores and deportment I had publicly criticized, as an equal.

Not likely. It was far easier to simply ignore them, which is what we did for the next month, as we approached the Red Planet.

♂ ♂ ♂

Mars loomed bright and full as we rose toward it from the sun. Our nuclear reactor shadow shields did double duty as we rode out a minor solar flare. In fact, it turned out that for the entire mission, the lowest total radiation dose was in the cabins right next to the reactor shield — because it stopped half the cosmic rays as well.

We learned later that the Norwegian ships had superconducting magnetic loops that channeled the proton influx harmlessly into their heat shield, behind their propellant tanks. Another "unproven" technology, but not only did it protect the Norwegians, but they actually gained a few centimeters per second push from the interaction of the charged particle storm with their magnetic field.

Little good would that do them! Doing midcourse maneuvers with our fleet is not trivial, but I found need for another one. I was a demon: I sold it to Dr. Worthing and pushed the planning through with two sets of books — the vector I intended to use would get us there a little earlier.

Four countdowns had to go perfectly, everything forty people have spread around had to be stowed, four computers needed to agree on everything — it takes days of planning. But under my leadership it went perfectly, and it added just enough delta-V to get us back ahead of the Norwegians without creating big political problems for Mission Control.

The "race," of course, had assumed David and Goliath proportions in the Earth media, and guess who was cast as Goliath? I was obliged to do interviews in which I decried any competition and said conciliatory things about "my colleague, Dr. Karinsdatter." When, as a result of our "nominal" and "planned" maneuver, we gradually pulled away from the Norwegians, the media cried foul. However, by that time, they could do nothing but throw words at us.

Not so Halvorsen. I was in my cabin ten days before our Mars orbit injection when the Norwegians threw us yet another twist. We watched it on the telescope, recorded it, and I'm still not sure I believe it: the Norwegian ships separated without despinning! The one on the approaching leg of its rotation just let go of its tether, and its rotational velocity instantly became additional velocity toward Mars! It was like a stone released from an ancient sling, headed right toward my heart.

I stared for five minutes, then played the file back again. "Give me the revised arrival times," I finally told the computer.

It was as bad as I feared. The lead ship, the *Amundsen,* had gained only about thirty meters per second, which would still leave it still more than a day behind us when we got to Mars. The trouble was that they were planning to go right down if they could, and we were going to do parking orbits, surveys, transfer to landers and so on, before actually going down. If all went right with both our plans, our first landings would take place within hours of each other — theirs first.

I stared at the screen and composed my thoughts for the next call. It would not be my place to educate the ISA leaders under whose authority I commanded this expedition, but the experienced astronaut within me was saying that the Norwegians had a chance. I needed to break the news gently.

At least, if their landing was successful, it would minimize the perturbations of our extremely complex and interrelated mission plan.

But on the other hand, our expedition would not be first, and I would not be the first man to set foot on Mars. Once more, I reviewed our mission plans, the Martian weather, where our landers were and so on. There was still a chance, *if* the lead Norwegian ship didn't touch down on the first pass. That, I thought, would depend on Per Nordli's skill and nerve.

Not exactly, as things turned out.

The simultaneous deep space restart of our nuclear rockets was ten times as complicated as the chemical midcourse maneuvers. but we did it without incident, silencing many critics. One after another, our ships turned their damping drums and their reactors went critical. A trickle of hydrogen flowed into the particle beds to cool them and run the turbines. The computers did a million cross checks. Deviations were within nominal limits.

We passed the orbit of Deimos — twenty thousand kilometers out — in good form. We would meet the moon itself, with our supply depot, after our main engine burn at periapsis put us in an elliptical transfer orbit. At Deimos, we'd do a short circularization burn with our chemical auxiliary propulsion and "land" on the tiny moon to take on propellant before sending landers to Mars. That was the plan.

Our Phobos camera sent a picture of our four ships with the volcanoes of Tharsis in the background; it was a spectacular picture. I felt a moment of triumph. Our majestic convoy, the symbol of Earth's pioneering spirit, was headed in to mankind's new planet!

This impressive close formation approach, however, had been another "discretionary" part of the mission plan. Originally, the ships were going to come in at one day intervals. But that would have meant another day before I reached the surface.

My moment of triumph was short-lived. Hours before, the *Amundsen* had made a final course correction — an expected maneuver given the chancy aerobraking ahead of it. But the trajectory report indicated that the *Amundsen* had actually done a major burn *toward* the planet! The burn had cut hours off its trajectory, but it would hit the Martian atmosphere at a slightly *higher* velocity, just an hour before our burn. So the Norwegians weren't racing? I thought about negative lift and velocity-squared aerodynamic effects and could guess that something besides the race might have lead them to this suicidal dive into the Martian atmosphere, but it wasn't very convincing. No, I decided, Per Nordli was taking this risk so Halvorsen wouldn't lose his diabolical little race.

Madre diablo! Given the way he managed all the other news about the expedition, couldn't Dr. Worthing have held *that* announcement back from us until we were safely in orbit?

But no. As we approached our eight-hundred kilometer periapsis, the *Amundsen* went past us, rounding the rim of the planet. We watched its entry on images from the robot telescopes on Deimos — a long trail of fire covering almost a quarter the circumference of the planet, which then winked out.

Had the *Amundsen* crashed? Had it burned up before reaching the surface? I both feared, and — forgive me — hoped that might be the case.

But no. We saw the landing pictures taken by an automated camera on the Norwegian supply ships and relayed from Earth just as we prepared for our insertion burn. Then there was that historic video from the cabin of the *Amundsen*.

When Halvorsen has a point to make, he doesn't go half way. Despite his talk of Per being better with piloting and trajectories, the first person to land on Mars with the Norwegian and United Nations flags on the side of her ship was Dr. Ingrid Bodil Karinsdatter.

"May their malfunctioning toilets line their vacuum tents with their own dung," Mustaffa muttered.

But other than that, there were just stony looks all through operations.

We were demoralized. We'd lost a race we hadn't known we were in until it was too late, and we'd lost it to someone we regarded as a bimbo. If you are European, perhaps you say, "So what? That's a juvenile attitude. Professional astronauts shouldn't be fazed by that." But most of my men were not from your culture; their pride had been wounded and their values insulted — and we still had a great many very complex things to do.

Spacecraft had to be prepared for thrust after four months of no gravity. Countless things were stowed. Chairs were moved to the aft bulkhead. A myriad of checklists were executed. Finally, the count reached zero.

On the *Chang-Diaz* a gentle thrumming vibration took hold, and a sense of down returned. There were disturbing clatters and crashes as things forgotten fell aft, but the thrust ramped up smoothly. The other ships kept pace and formation. I crossed my fingers and hoped the blow to our morale would have no effect, at least not now.

Perhaps it would have made no difference, but perhaps if the crew of the *Leonov* had been mentally and emotionally sharp, they would not have missed some things and a water bulb would not have fallen from the sill of a viewport and broken on a relay box that should have been closed, soaking its contents as thrust increased.

And the pilot would not have switched circuits to their back-ups in exactly the wrong order, causing the *Leonov*'s lander to separate when deceleration built up to half a gee.

And the lander would not have continued forward to strike the decelerating *Calypso*.

And the suddenly lighter *Leonov* would not have moved backward relative to the *Clarke* and into the exhaust of the latter's nuclear rocket.

And the radiation level monitors aboard the *Leonov* would not have shut down their reactor before they had braked into the proper orbit, forcing them to complete the burn with what remained of their maneuvering fuel.

And the *Clarke*'s computer would not have shut down *their* engine to avoid endangering the *Leonov* when it found the latter spacecraft in its exhaust cone.

Carumba! Perhaps something like that would have all happened anyway, as Halvorsen anticipated, because of the complexity. But I think it was because we were on edge, unhappy at losing the "race," and already dreaming about getting home.

The *Calypso*'s chemical propellant tanks ruptured, but they somehow retained attitude control by gimballing the main engine, avoided hitting the Martian atmosphere, and limped into a high equatorial orbit. Mustaffa cut our burn short manually to follow them, and using prodigious quantities of our maneuvering fuel we managed a rendezvous.

Pierre, Ramon, and Mustaffa went out in vacuum suits, and managed to bring the six survivors over before their leaking hull finally gave way.

So the rescue was an epic of astronautics, but it left the *Calypso* ruined and the *Chang-Diaz* in a too-large eccentric orbit with almost no chemical propellant left. Rendezvous with the supply depot was now impossible.

The *Clarke*'s maneuver had been stopped short of capture and they now had to take the emergency return trajectory back to Earth. The name of the ship's commander was Roger Moses — another irony. But the *Leonov* did manage its rendezvous with Deimos and the supply depot — one out of four. By the time Mission Control and my staff had straightened everything out, we had lost two days of schedule time, two spacecraft, and three landers, including both wheeled surface vehicles.

And where was Per Nordli? He was ten hours behind in the other Norwegian ship, the *Fram*. Halvorsen had told me they had their own redundancies and were not relying on us. I had not thought that through, but now it made sense that the better pilot come in second, in case a rescue was needed. He demonstrated his mastery by declining a one shot landing; he skipped out into a long elliptical orbit that matched ours, and offered assistance. But Mission Control determined that there was nothing his little ship could do.

Meanwhile, some of the *Leonov*'s crew reported exceeding their radiation limits and the doctors recommended that they go to the surface or return now. They voted to stay.

Perhaps we should have aborted the mission entirely, but I railed against this. To come so far...

No! I was a whirlwind of orders. We would fight back from disaster. We launched all our automated probes, balloons, and teleoperated rovers at once. They sped toward Mars well ahead of us, and data started streaming in as we passed the atmosphere-grazing periapsis of our orbit. Good news started to displace bad news.

Dr. Worthing sent out press releases that emphasized the redundancy built into the mission and the superior technical equipment in the United Nations landers versus those of the Norwegians. We expressed great sadness for our casualties, but dedicated the remaining mission to them.

I took risks. The *Chang-Diaz* was trapped in an unusable orbit, but had a usable lander. My staff came up with a brilliant improvisation: The *Chang-Diaz* lander could do an atmosphere-assisted orbit change to rendezvous with Deimos and the *Leonov*.

Once at Deimos, the lander could take on fuel and that would at least give us the *option* of a landing. Since there was no point any longer in pretending that such maneuvers were too uncertain for manned spacecraft, Mission Control quietly acceded — just in time for us to follow our fleet of drones into the atmosphere on that first periapsis.

Within twenty-four hours, we had a fueled lander ready to go. But Mission Control still objected to a one-lander surface mission in such circumstances.

So I went up to the political level to postpone a negative decision — no need to admit failure yet. A good face was put on everything as I worked furiously to get myself and some volunteers down to the planet. Of course, there were some minor drawbacks that never made the press releases. All that superior equipment was not on that one lander. The one that survived had an aircraft instead of a rover; so once we got there, we would have to walk where we couldn't fly.

Thirty hours after her landing, we watched Dr. Karinsdatter step off an *Amundsen* landing pad to gather samples. This told us that the Norwegian expedition had succeeded to that point, and put the final nail in the coffin of any remaining hopes for us — no one from our expedition would be the first person to set foot on Mars. A woman, instead, would join Gagarin and Armstrong in the history of space. My country once had such a woman as its Presidente. It was not a successful experiment.

Boris Yakov, the *Leonov*'s commander salvaged some glory for us. He went outside and left a footprint on Deimos.

Meanwhile, Dr. Karinsdatter roamed around her camp on the Martian surface in a pedal-powered, wire-wheeled tricycle, collected multitudinous samples, released some mini-balloons and transmitted a fair amount of surface data to that radio telescope north of Oslo herself.

Never mind the dollars per bit; our army of robot floaters and crawlers got far more data in absolute terms, and that is still coming in. We won in what counted.

We learned that one of the Norwegian supply landers had fallen into a sinkhole, and we made much of this with offers of assistance to Halvorsen. The answer came back that he thought no assistance was needed, but that we should talk directly to the people on the scene.

Finally, two days after we braked into orbit I declared the remaining lander ready for the descent. We were determined to make one quick strike for the goal. The public, the politicians, and ourselves would feel like failures if we didn't.

Five of us went down instead of the seven the mission plan called for. We said we had to do this to leave room for the Norwegians whom we might have to rescue — but in reality, four of the seven Leonov personnel with ground training asked to not be included in a one-lander mission. Despite their radiation exposure levels, they felt the slight protection of the Martian atmosphere was not worth the additional risk. Mission control did not dispute this.

At last I called Dr. Karinsdatter on the surface. Her base computer answered and the view from its comm camera filled my screen. It was a late Martian summer evening and I could see rolling hills and the dusty red horizon through their transparent inflated dome. For a moment, all the problems went away. This was why I had come.

"Commander Lopez?" Her voice came from off camera.

"*Sí*. I was admiring the view. We are going to descend in six hours, at local dawn. Is there anything you need?"

She walked up to the commset with a Martian rock in her hands. She had apparently just come in from sample gathering. Her hair, matted and disheveled was still tied behind her head in a pony tail that fell to her shoulder blades and she was wearing only the thin body stocking the Norwegians used under their tight vacuum suits. It both covered her completely and revealed everything — and she seemed utterly oblivious to what effect this might have on us.

Mixed feelings ran through me, and eventually resolved themselves into anger. I saw a brief frown of puzzlement go across her face as she reacted to my expression.

"Cover yourself," I demanded. "This circuit is open to my crew, who have not seen a woman in over six months."

She shrugged her shoulders. "That is not my fault." There was little soundproofing in our ships and I heard the men's reaction. "Perhaps they would enjoy seeing me then, Commander. But very well." The picture disappeared and I lost both Venus and Mars in one instant of self-inflicted pain. "At any rate, Commander," she continued, voice only, "this is an independent and self-sufficient expedition and we will get along better if you do not try to give me orders."

I ignored this challenge and went to business. "We will come in from the west, from over Kasei Vallis."

"*Ja*," she answered, seriously. "Beware — the ground here is crusty with cavities beneath. We had one supply lander tilt because of that. You may wish to land south of our position — we have traversed the area several times and the ground... it is mostly solid there."

I was irritated and unthinking. "We will make our own evaluation. If you continue to insist that you are in no need of our assistance, then I see little point in continuing contacts which would only be uncomfortable for both of us, I assure you."

She ignored the taunt. "Per and the *Fram* will be arriving in four hours — you have the vector?"

"Yes." Halvorsen and Worthing had buried some hatchets, and information was flowing now. "Give Per Nordli, my regards... and my sympathies."

"Commander, I regret any affront I've given you. Please, when you land, we will welcome you. I take no offense. Is this understood?"

Somewhere in the back of my mind, warning bells began to ring. Best not burn bridges. Christ allowed such a woman to wash His feet, I remembered belatedly. But that woman was repentant.

"Very well." In the end, Thy will, not mine, be done. "I shall do what I need to do to bring back as many of us and as much data as I can. Rest assured of that, Dr. Karinsdatter. Lopez out."

"*Lykke til*, Commander. Luck to you."

We would have to do all our ground exploring by foot, I thought. I did not want to take Norwegian leftovers, so we would have to traverse new ground. That way we would gain unique data and perhaps, hope against hope, find something which they had not found.

I put it that way to Mission Control. They told me 'no,' land where the people on the ground say.

Did they take me for a child? I appealed to the political level again and got my way. I had not yet learned humility. That lesson came five hours later.

♂ ♂ ♂

We came in north of the Norwegians, in an uncratered area that was free of their tracks. Our computer gave us a textbook, fuzzy-logic-smooth landing, and I congratulated myself for not having to touch anything. It was not so bad, I told myself. Erikson had been five hundred years ahead of Columbus, Amundsen a month ahead of Scott, but we had closed the gap to a couple of days.

Then a patch of thin crust gave in under the weight of our plus-zed landing leg and our fuel-laden lander tilted, stopping sharply when the unsupported leg hit the permafrost under the dust crust. A strut bent upward under redline stress, snapped, and impaled an oxidizer tank with its upper ten centimeters. Red fuming nitric acid flowed onto the already well-oxidized Martian soil and reacted in a way that produced more smoke than heat. But it looked spectacular.

Without pressure in the tank to hold it against the lander cabin's Earth-normal atmosphere, the lander floor bent down, and cracked. Our escaping air vibrated the sides of the crack like a monster oboe reed as it escaped, to be replaced by nitric acid fumes. It sounded, felt, and smelled like hell.

With the fortune of prudent and well-rehearsed planning, we were wearing our spacesuits so we were not immediately harmed. I blew the lock doors and led the crew out onto the red soil away from the lander, in case there was an explosion. But no, the oxidizer just ran out and fizzled as we watched.

"Enrico," Mustaffa said later, in an unfortunate attempt to lighten my mood, "at least this makes you the first *man* to set foot on Mars."

The spacecraft shuddered and settled again. We watched helplessly as our two-man aircraft pulled free of its upper latch and pivoted down, breaking its back when its nose slammed into the ocher soil.

My look must have been as cold as the permafrost outside.

"My apologies, Commander," he said quickly, after he saw my face.

Unfortunately, since the lander used the oxidizer to fuel its generator, and the battery leads were cut when the floor buckled, our power was gone. Our communications plan did not call for spacesuit-to-orbit communications. The plan was to relay communications through the lander, which had triply redundant transmitters. In the impossible event of a triple failure on one lander, the backup was to relay through the another lander — the one that was now on its way back to Earth in the *Clarke*.

Per Nordli's *Fram* came in overhead as we milled around our stricken lander. We could actually hear the ticks of his sonic boom — reminding us that we were on a planet with some atmosphere. We waved up at him like mad monkeys, but he was gone in a moment, over our horizon, far ahead of his shock wave. So now there were three manned spacecraft on Mars. Even in those circumstances, I took time to wonder at what we had been allowed to accomplish, and give thanks.

It was into the early afternoon before we gave up on trying to revive any of the lander's systems. We had suit battery power for about three more hours. We could walk in the suits without power for a little longer than that, straining against the air pressure in a kind of penguin shuffle. Our air could last a little longer than the batteries but not much.

The only choice we had was to try to trek to the Norwegian base. They couldn't see our problem, because, of course, we had taken pains to land ourselves just below their horizon. We couldn't radio them. No matter — our digital suit radios were encrypted for privacy. I briefly considered trying to telegraph some kind of primitive code by cycling my transponder — but I didn't know one.

It was a long walk, even in four-tenths of a gravity. Our suits were heavy, and we had to be very sparing of the power assist. We were all tired, scruffy and unwashed. A few were injured. Some of us exceeded the capacity of the waste management systems built into some of our suits. I shall not try to describe the way we smelled. We didn't know if anyone else in the universe knew we were still alive.

The historical parallels are endless, and great fun, I know. I led the bigger, more expensive, and more technologically advanced expedition, but I ended up seeing just what Scott saw. I think I understood the mixed feelings Scott must have felt as he approached the south pole in the last century when I saw the white-bordered blue cross on a red field painted high on the side of one of the *Fram's* tanks.

That flag had signified both the failure to be *numero uno*, and the success of gaining his goal to Scott as well. It was in such a mental state that I approached the inflated plastic dome of the Norwegian base as the frigid Martian night began to descend on us. Our power was giving out, cold was seeping in, pride was gone, and there was only the business of survival.

The Norwegian base was half a kilometer from their ships, and it was a mess. Pieces of the partly dissembled supply landers lay strewn about. There were hoses going this way and that. Empty containers lay were they had been unpacked. They seemed to have put little time into being tidy. On the other hand, there may have been a pragmatic purposefulness about the seeming clutter — anything important was in plain view and could be reached directly from their dome's air lock.

The transparent dome was double walled, and within that was a small white tent which seemed to be under positive pressure. It was also moving gently back and forth — clearly, we were not expected.

But we were running out of air, and there was nothing to do but bang very hard on the outer airlock door. A trillion dollars, twenty nations, thirty-two men, and eleven months in space had come down to this moment of low comedy as our group of five desperate beggars shuffled like arthritic penguins up to someone else's door. I did not quite appreciate it then — I was freezing and tired.

The Norwegians thought something was wrong with their equipment and responded to the noise immediately in hurriedly donned pressure gear, helmets in hand. Dr. Karinsdatter came out of the tent first. She clearly wasn't expecting to see us and the power assisted hard suits look somewhat alien at first glance. It must have taken her a minute to close her mouth and open the outer air lock door.

I came through last, as was my privilege. Strangely, I did not start shaking uncontrollably until I was out of the frigid suit and into the warm air of the Norwegian base. But what keeps going through my mind is not the low comedy, but the sad, haunting, melody I heard as I came in from their airlock to safety. Grieg, of course. Solveig's song, which will always be Ingrid's song, to me. It matched my mood of remorse and humiliation.

♂ ♂ ♂

By midnight, we had rigged emergency sleep sacks for my men from mylar blankets glued edge to edge, and settled them just inside the west perimeter of the dome. We ate a meal of reconstituted pasta and meat sauce that tasted extraordinarily good, as any meal will under such circumstances. I took a stimulant, notified our surprised colleagues in orbit that I was still alive, and began to analyze the situation and had begun to evolve a course of action — but the next thing I knew, I was turning over under a blanket and it was morning. Dr. Karinsdatter was hovering over me with a communicator.

I found my embarrassment at begging shelter in the Norwegians' love nest was nothing compared to what happened on Earth while I was asleep. Dr. Worthing's initial effort to have the U.N. take over command of Halvorsen's mission was resolved when Secretary-General Ryskoff secured Dr. Worthing's resignation and put Halvorsen in charge of both missions. Halvorsen found out which department heads could still fit into engineering hats and put them to work with their people to get us back safely. The others stood aside and watched.

Per thought that he had enough tools to fix our lander, if we could get fuel to it. But they were using carbon monoxide and liquid oxygen, while we were using hydrazine and nitric acid.

To find out that this had been a consideration of Halvorsen's from the start was another suitable lesson in humility for me. He had designed the *Amundsen* and the *Fram*, as much as anything else, as a lifeboats for *us*, in anticipation of our failure. So much for one problem.

But once back in Mars orbit, we would have face the fact that we had, essentially, two and a half U. N. crews and two U. N. ships, one stuck out in an unuseful orbit almost out of maneuvering fuel. While Dr. Karinsdatter was seeing to my crew, I spoke to Per.

"My plan had been to take the lander back to the *Chang-Diaz* and transship propellant from our supply depot. But that lander will not fly again. Can the *Amundsen* ferry fuel?"

"*Nei*. To go out to Deimos, circularize, then go back towing a large mass so we cannot aerobrake, and then burn back to Earth? We do not have enough fuel for that. The *Chang-Diaz* has its nuclear engine, why not use that?"

"The design is for only two more restarts, maybe three in a crunch. It's a thermal cycling limit — after six or seven cycles the inner frit starts to crack. It was a trade that let them make the engines lighter and more powerful — they only needed four burns. So a main orbit transfer maneuver would need two more restarts which would likely lead to engine failure during an Earth arrival maneuver."

"*Ja*." Per smiled at me, this man whose only passion seemed to be this kind of technical problem, and that passion a mild one, "but you still have the reactor on the *Leonov*, powerful enough, I think, to get you all back. And you have the fuel and crew modules on the *Chang-Diaz*. So, how do we now put all these pieces together?"

We spent the day with computers, drawing screens, and stylus and came up with a plan to send to Halvorsen. We left it with the Norwegians' computer to send, then turned in.

Halvorsen then called me in the middle of the Martian night on one of the spare comm units the Norwegians had given me. The man could do a clinic on revenge, I think. I got some minor satisfaction by getting Per up to hear it too.

"Okay," he began once I was coherent. "Your *Chang-Diaz* uses its main engines to push itself and the *Leonov* to almost rendezvous with the supply cache, then separates the reactor module. Then you complete the docking with chemical rockets. You fuel both ships, then you depart using the *Leonov's* nuclear engine."

Per joined me, as blurry-eyed as I was. The inside of the dome was warm with bodies, overloading the Norwegians' small recycler — I smelled not only my own body but everyone else's.

We were all down to shorts.

"*Sí*." I told Halvorsen. "Its engine can get both spacecraft to Earth if it can use the fuel left in the *Chang-Diaz* as well as its own." This much Per and I had discussed.

"But, Dr. Halvorsen, to make this work, the fuel remaining in the *Chang-Diaz* has to be pumped into to the *Leonov* and we can't pump under zero gravity. We must use the reaction control thrusters, or the weak gravity of Deimos to settle the propellant first. Once under thrust, the pumps work. But now we don't have enough reaction control fuel to sustain that much pumping time. Over." Minutes passed as I regretted using up my extra margin in the vain effort to get to Mars first.

Finally, Halvorsen's answer arrived: "*Ja*. Your technicians said that was the only way to pump fuel. But then they said it can't be done under main engine thrust because of where the thrust vector would have to be with the ships tied together. You have to gimbal the *Leonov's* engine hard right, to put the thrust line through the center of mass, but the pump will shut down if the gimbal is more than five degrees, no? A safety measure."

I remember those cold blue eyes staring at me from the screen.

"*Uflaks*. So you have to think harder. I think you know now well enough to look beyond what things were designed to do to see what they *can* do. And I think you know now well enough to learn from others, without it hurting your manhood. We are all tied together now, *nei*? It would be most helpful for you to solve this problem yourself for your self-respect and that of your crew. Their morale is tied to yours. So now you think and you think hard. Tomorrow, you tell me what you think. Halvorsen out."

"*Uff*. I think better morning," Per said, "good nights."

Learn from others, Halvorsen said. Tied together. Think hard. I inflated my mattress, removed everything but my shorts and crawled into my bag without remembering that I had done so.

I thought. The Norwegians used tethers to give themselves gravity during the mission coast phase. Fuel transfer required acceleration — which was not necessarily thrust. Our ships were not built for rotating around each other on tethers. Where would one attach them? Impossible.

I did what I have done since a child to clear my mind. I prayed. Lord deliver me. Some call it a retreat to a fantasy world, a land of childhood faith in tooth fairies and Easter bunnies. If so, why is it still so strong in me, as other illusions have dropped away? That I do not know. But I do know the absence from here and now settles my mind.

An image came to my mind almost unbidden. I remembered watching the ships being hoisted up to their stations on top of the heavy lift vehicle. There were hard points in the noses where one could attach cables. Tethers. Just a little rotation would do for the fuel transfer, and, I thought, the system might be strong enough to give my crew some artificial gravity on the way back. I rolled out of the sack and headed for the terminals on the other side of the dome.

I found Ingrid still working, under red night-vision lighting, packing samples for the morning's departure at a flimsy looking bench opposite their tent. She wore shorts and a thin, dusty t-shirt. Not really understanding what was happening to me, I explained my idea with a breathlessness that had little to do with the mental effort.

"Not so difficult." She smiled. "We have spare tethers and hosing which we no longer need here."

The smile did it. She was lean, smooth, intense, glowing with health. She put a hand lightly on my arm. "Are you all right? You have been under much strain, I think."

God help me, I just put my arms around her, my head on her shoulder and moaned. If I had done that at NASA, I would have been reported. But she made no objection. After a minute, she gave a slight low laugh. returned my hug, and rocked me back and forth like a child. Urgency overcame me. My hands found their way down her back and beneath the elastic of her shorts.

"Are you trying to seduce me?" She asked, in a voice that neither invited or condemned, but seemed more in the tone of curiosity.

My men were wrapped in emergency blankets sleeping on the other side of the dome. Per was asleep in the tent. She could have yelled and destroyed me, humiliating me even beyond anything that had happened so far, I was that far out of line — and I could not help myself, not even for a moment.

But instead of acting offended, she stroked me gently, "I do not mind." she murmured. "Per is sometimes too polite." She knelt to the floor and I followed. Her kisses were light and motherly at first, then more and more passionate. And so we two responsible adults made love, then and there, as if we were teenagers in the back seat of a car.

All through it, she smiled at me as if I were a child she was indulging with a minor treat. And when it was over, I turned my head so that she would not see my tears. But she pressed my head to herself and held me again as a mother would a child.

"This is nothing wrong," she murmured, as my sobs turned into deep breaths. "We both need this, so do not hate yourself for it. But now we must work on getting people back to Earth, yes?"

Six sleepless hours of calls to Mission Control later, our engineers had conceded that the remaining crews could have some gravity on the way back — with the *Leonov* and the *Chang-Diaz* tethered nose to nose. Fortunately, the U.N. ships were launched as fuel tanks with their interiors fitted afterwards — they could be rearranged for spin gravity from inside and that would give their crews something to do. The thermal control people griped, the communications people griped, the propulsion people smiled.

And the numbers worked out, just. We would have to put everyone on the *Leonov* before the final Earth orbit capture burn, and discard the *Chang-Diaz*, but my ship would have served its purpose as lifeboat and fuel tank by that time.

But the *Amundsen* and *Fram* were designed to go directly to Earth, on a faster trajectory. The easiest thing to do was to not try for a rendezvous, but rather for those of us on the surface to stay with the Norwegians. I relinquished my diminished command to Boris Yakov on *Leonov* and watched the ticklish tether and departure operations from the surface. This was my penance for my pride.

Three of my men lifted out on the *Amundsen* with Ingrid while I and another lifted with Per on the *Fram*. We passed Phobos on the way out — the inner Martian moon would have to wait.

We tethered together without incident after trans-Earth insertion in an operation that turned out to be surprisingly simple. Per went outside and hooked the ships together while they were nosed up to each other. Each ship then translated to its own right while the line played out, and when the cable was mostly out, did a small burn at right angles to the tether to induce the rotation. Any swinging motions were damped with attitude control thrusters.

Despite six men and one woman, there were no struggles between people on the return mission. Its Commander and her understanding first mate saw to that. The Norwegians had a little battery powered tether runner that gripped the line like a set of tram wheels and pulled you from one ship to another. Ingrid made the trip once a week. We all had frequent times alone with her — and it was not necessarily for sex. People are made to come in pairs, I think, and there are times when it is comforting to be with a woman even if you do nothing but look at the stars, not even talk.

One night three weeks out from Mars, we found ourselves in the dome alone. Per and Mustaffa were asleep below. We sat side by side on one of the acceleration couches, touching comfortably — and uncomfortably. I was fighting a war with myself inside, and losing, again.

"Could you care for me, really." I asked, meaning could you be the wife of a man who would protect you, who would not let you sleep with others, who would lead you instead of follow? "I think, at times, that I would undo everything to have you, and accept what fate that would bring."

To take another man's wife? To steal in the bed a share of the glory I could not win among the stars? No man with self-respect would do that, but events had stripped me to my essential needs. I could summon little sympathy for Per either; he seemed far too careless with his property.

Ingrid touched my lips with her fingers. "It could not be the same with you as with Per. He gives me the space I need and, in my way, I am unbreakably loyal to him. I enjoy doing things for people I care for, but not for life. I cannot be owned by anyone, and I think you want to own me."

Wanting what I cannot have is a way of life for me. It does not stop me from trying. I looked up at the *Amundsen*, far overhead on the other end of the tether. "Does it have a telescope?" I asked.

"Of course it does," she answered, "do you think they watch us now?" She smiled and waved at the distant ship. "Should we put on a show?"

I shook my head. "Ingrid, God forgive me, I want to love you, but to prove it, you ask me to abandon my culture, my concepts of right and wrong that lie more deeply in my soul than any other. I am ashamed of myself."

"I am not ashamed of what I do not think is wrong." She smiled and added, "But I would not embarrass you. We can always turn out the lights, Enrico, so no one can see through the reflection."

I stared at her. "You knew."

"I know many things — like how to win a race to Mars, and how to run a happy ship."

"The maneuvers, the surprise separation. That wasn't Halvorsen's doing?"

"Was Halvorsen on this ship? Was it Halvorsen who had a personal stake in being first? Oh, he had point to make, but, *nei*, it was not a point that required his being first. If anything he is somewhat upset." Her laugh was a throaty burble of delight. "No, that dear old man did not beat you to Mars. I did. I wanted to be first because I am a woman and I wanted to do something no one would ever forget, or put in second place. So I did it."

The look of complete shock on my face must have troubled even her. Good men had died — but did they die because of what she did, or because of what I did in response? And if she had not responded and it had happened anyway — I and five more would be dead.

"You must get used to this, I think." She caressed my chest and murmured, "It is not so hard to understand, is it? That no one owns me, that I, too, pursue my own goals and my own happiness?"

But it was hard. My mind was elsewhere, so lost in the maze of contingency that the only way out was to step out of the maze entirely through a greater dimension — that of providence. What happened, happened. It was not my fate to be first in anything — on Mars, or in the heart of the woman I must love, and hate, more than any other. Finally I took solace in how far from being last in all these things I was.

"I should die for this," I said before my lips met hers for what I vowed would be the last time. "Or you. I am not sure who."

♂ ♂ ♂

I did not gain the reward of death during the aerocapture maneuver when the *Amundsen* reached Earth, and I had to endure the purgatory of weeks and months of impoliteness from the insatiable vampires of the media. I fled to southernmost Argentina. Per and Ingrid went to Mars twice more, and settled there in 2043.

I have not been into space again — no one has asked for me, and I have not tried. I will not tempt providence again. Linda and I settled on a ranchero near Rio Gallegos. It is a cold, bitter land but suitable for cattle, horses, and grandchildren.

Over the years, with agonizing slowness, this sleazy badgering of the press has dribbled down to the point that I almost miss it, as one might miss the pain of an aching joint that becomes so familiar as to be part of one's personality. The fact of my being part of that first group to go to Mars has assumed more importance, and the circumstances less and less.

And, in the bottom of a desk drawer among things my late wife never saw, I keep an old picture of Ingrid, clipped from one of those magazines whose photographers had caught Ingrid on the Riviera so many years ago. In shame, I look at it and remember. I look at it and wonder, is she our future? There are many like her in space these days, and some who see a biological aspect to these things point out that the mind-set best for managing a spacecraft is very close to that of keeping a home.

I dare think now that my male-oriented values, my ideas of a paternal God, my beliefs of what men and women should be, may not fit out there as well as hers. Such beliefs may be of no more lasting consequence than those of the people who built the pyramids or crossed the Bering Strait. Save for these past few primitive centuries, Ingrid Karinsdatter's way of loving and living may be what most of eternity thinks of as typically human.

Still, the pyramids are there. I salute their builders.

Looking back, the wonder may be not that a big, complicated, political, hierarchal UN/ISA mission was beaten to Mars by a woman, but that there was one at all.

Forgive me; but when I look on Ingrid, I still long for something. But it is not a body or a moment of illicit joy that time can never return that I covet as I contemplate the possibilities of eternity. No, it is not *her* that I covet. Not her so much as her freedom.

AFTERWORD — MARTIAN VALKYRIE

THIS WAS MY RESPONSE to a panel discussion question at a science fiction convention some years ago, when someone maintained that one couldn't do a Mars mission without nuclear rockets.

Personally, I think nuclear rockets are a good idea. They are not particularly dangerous by the standards of space travel and their immense propulsion capacity would be a net safety factor, allowing more supplies per traveler, faster trips with less exposure to cosmic radiation. As a bonus, you'd get a high quality power supply at the destination.

But they are not necessary to go to Mars — six kilometers per second and an aerobraking system will get you to the Martian surface — about the same velocity change needed to get into geosynchronous orbit. Once there, you can make your own fuel for the return.

Recently, there was an attempt by three teams to float balloons around the world. The only one that made any significant progress was the simple version, with a single pilot.

The trajectories for this turned out to be somewhat faster versions of those used by the two U.S. Spacecraft headed for Mars at this writing. One, the Global Surveyor, is taking the traditional near-Hohmann path, a minimum velocity change trajectory which just touches, in its ideal form, the orbits of the two objects it travels between. It will perform a large breaking and capture maneuver when it reaches its closest point to Mars, but will subsequently do some aerobraking to modify its orbit.

The other spacecraft, the Pathfinder, will precede the path of Ingrid Karinsdatter, using the Martian atmosphere for rendezvous, capture, and descent. It is also following a significantly faster trajectory. If you are not too concerned about the relative velocity when you encounter the planet, for just a little more velocity change than a Hohmann transfer orbit, you can save months of transit time. The resulting orbit intersects the Martian orbit at an angle, and you need to get rid of more relative velocity when you get there, but that's what the Martian atmosphere was put there for, wasn't it?

The Mars Global Surveyor was launched with a Delta, the same kind of rocket that puts communications satellites in orbit. One needs to watch out for variation in the density of the Martian atmosphere, and if you need to go low to get enough of it, you need to watch out for those big volcanoes as well. But those are manageable problems, particularly when you save months and tens of millions of dollars' worth of launch costs to get there.

A personal note. I had enough fun with the Norwegian explorational character in this story that I thought I should make it clear that I was of Norwegian descent myself — and that was the reason for "Per Nordli," using the traditional spelling. I don't know Norwegian myself, but in addition to Stan Schmidt holding my feet to the fire on the spelling, I had some good help from the family.

And, finally, I should note with a little ethnic pride that Norway *is* starting to stick its nose into the space business, taking care of the sea end of the "Sea Launch" private space transportation effort.

A WORLD TO SHARE

HIVE-LORD ALTHOR could now stand on the Planet without assistance from mechanical things. Their archeological dig had stirred up enough ancient dust that the thin wisps of remaining atmosphere turned red at sunset — a cold beautiful red that spoke of empty shores and peace. But all things come to an end. A dozen daughters were brooding on various space colonies, soon to become Hive Lords themselves. They would carry on the work. For him, well, he had always intended to return, and the starship was near ready.

"Then we are done, Eldest Daughter?"

He still called her that, though with the delivery of her first brood, her sex change was well underway. Calling her that helped avoid those uncomfortable male-male feelings.

"Hive-Father, the pickings have been very slim, but almost a dozen species have lived here at one time or another, and at least three have arisen here. There are records of something buried deep in the innermost moon — a time capsule maybe — we're just starting to look there. The world seems to have been tended; there is little evidence of war or any major conflict between species, as far as I can tell. The older ones quietly moved on when the newer ones were ready, though sometimes they persisted in the myths and legends of the newer species."

"As we might someday. Well, continue your work then. I leave this world with, shall we say, a perspective... yes, an altered perspective. Time... there is so much time."

A fireball glowed in the evening, streaking overhead to the west, moving, he thought, and surprisingly slowly.

"Hive-Father," his robots called, "A spacecraft approaches, and not one of ours. It came from the innermost moon. The whole core of the moon came electromagnetically alive as soon as we started digging."

Eldest Daughter adopted a tentacles akimbo posture of astonishment that must have matched his own. "What have we let loose? Hive-Father... we've been digging in someone's graveyard."

Althor willed his one tentacles to stop quivering. Whatever it was, it was clearly obeying the same laws of space, time and energy as the rest of the universe. It would take them a few minutes at least to arrive.

"Who or whatever it is, I expect they are wise with age and deep in tolerance, else we would have been roasted in our shells already. Prepare yourself to act with dignity."

And so Althor and Eldest Daughter stood calmly when a plume of dust announced the arrival of the spacecraft. And they remained calm when the strange dark biped in a shiny black spacesuit walked over their tailings and came toward them.

But it was still a surprise to see not one of the last of the world's inhabitants, but the first.

Dressed in vacuum gear, they were not ugly. And this one's face behind its visor, animated with protuberances as it was, seemed almost normal to Althor now. It stopped a body length from them — one of theirs, two of its, and addressed them in their own language.

Of course. Hive-Lord Althor knew now that for all his planet's starships and progress, he and it were but a day old bud in the nursery of the universe. He trembled, but was not ashamed to tremble before this.

"Hello," it said in firm tones, yet with a hint of gentleness to them. "My name is Ingrid, and this is my planet..." The being bared its teeth — but then did as credible an imitation of the gesture of good feeling as could be done with two stiff limbs.

"...but I share."

ACKNOWLEDGEMENTS

"**M**orning on Mars" and "The Day of Their Coming" were written in my first year as a writer while I was still living in the tiny desert town of Boron, California. I had no writer's group to look at my stories then, and not even my wife, who had moved north to seek work with Apple Computer. So I relied on my friend and neighbor, Dawn Minette, a retired mining engineer and science fiction fan, for critiques and proofreading. She will always have a very special place in my heart.

Then, when I moved north to be with Gayle, I joined my present writers groups, which have over the last five years included many people, some better known than others. If I were to attempt to reconstruct who read which stories and offered what criticism, I would inevitably leave someone out. So they are all hereby thanked collectively and anonymously.

Last but not least, I should acknowledge the encouragement and efforts of my editor, Bridgett McKenna of Scorpius Digital Publishing and, for the latest edition, of Deb Houdek of Variations on a Theme.

Visit
briefcandlepress.com
to read about the author,
upcoming publications,
and articles about
the science behind the stories